I0606645

Connivance
History of Sol 4
Steven Dutch, Chris Masterton

Masterton Dutch Multimedia

History of Sol

Book 4: First Edition

ii

Written by

Steven Dutch & Chris Masterton

Edited by

Mick

Cover art by

Jason Giraldo

Cover design and formatting by

Chris Masterton

Copyright © 2024

Steven Dutch & Chris Masterton

All rights reserved.

This story, as far as we know, is entirely a work of fiction. Perhaps we have inadvertently channelled these tales from the distant future. Perhaps it has been sent back to us by some powerful being, as a warning of things to come. We cannot be sure. But what we do know is, that the names, characters and incidents portrayed throughout this story are the work of the authors' imaginations. Any resemblance to actual persons, living or dead is entirely coincidental. This story, its characters and artworks are the intellectual property of Chris Masterton & Steven Dutch. No part of this publication may be reproduced, stored in a retrieval system or transmitted in any form or by any means, electronic, mechanical, telepathic, photocopy, recording or otherwise, without prior permission.

Acknowledgements

This book has been a long time in the making, so the first thanks go to everyone who has been continually pestering—I mean patiently waiting—and asking us if we're still working on it. Well, here it is!

One man was instrumental in ensuring this came together by keeping us accountable, offering direction, and outright berating us until we got it right. Thanks, Mick, for all your wisdom and encouragement.

Jason is the phenomenal artist responsible for the cover and internal artworks. Thanks, as always, for your ongoing dedication to our vision.

We gave the manuscript to Johnny a few weeks before publication and asked him to review it with an eagle's eye, which he did quickly and enthusiastically. Thanks for noticing (and fixing) all our typos.

Lastly, thanks to our supportive partners, Rach and Yani, who allow us to sit on our computers all day and talk shit while pretending to be productive writers.

DATAFILE
UAEN Elysium

NODE 1

The United Advancement Entity Navy *Elysium* is a Heavy Destroyer (Lunar-Class) constructed on *M6 Orbital Space Station*. It's operation responsibilities include: protection of Colonial space and assets, suppression of outlaw activities, and maintenance of regional stability.

NODE 2

The *Elysium* is a high-performance, multi-mission warship designed to execute standalone patrol operations in defence of the Lunar Colony's territorial borders. Of its many functions, this class of Destroyer is primarily used to escort larger vessels in a fleet, or act alone to enforce the strict ban on travelling through the Terranean Expanse.

The ship was reassigned in C1099 to the UAEN as part of a tribute announced by The Nexus to bolster a military presence around the outer planets.

NODE 3

The Elysium's advanced armament and hull design make it an effective and resilient asset for defence and enforcement operations. Its optimised interfaces allow it to be operated by a crew of fifty officers, and accommodates a further complement of one hundred marines for boarding operations.

Primary armaments include thirty-six hull-mounted turrets that shoot self-propelled smart rounds, eight missile tubes and twelve multi-directional particle beam cannons.

The hull is made up of Dual-Layer Titanium Alloy (DLTA) with an interlayer of Gel-Based Self-Sealing Membrane (GSSM) that restores almost instantly when penetrated.

CHAPTER ONE
Elysium - C1099 S5 R2

Kedric glanced at the time index on his workstation. Three hours into his shift, and not even a rock to shoot at, much less the outlaws he was there to fight. The mission statement of the United Advancement Entity was to protect the Colonies against rogue factions. But so far on the UAEN *Elysium*, they hadn't encountered a single one. Instead, they were running errands for the Mars Colony, moving freight to some unknown research facility. He looked over at Dewitt, briefly watched as the helmsman ran a docking simulator on his station.

An alert sounded from the ops console and Clydeman reported. "XO, you might want to take a look at this. I'm picking up two ships, fast inbound, no transponders."

The XO, Girbach, sat up in his chair. "Hostiles? How far?"

"They're eighty thousand kiltrons and closing," Clydeman said. "Heat signatures suggest weapons are active."

"Prepare to engage."

An alert thrummed through the control room, but Kedric barely heard it. He was already focused on the tactical scope. His heart rate doubled. This was it. They were finally going to see some action. He locked his chair into the console and brought up the scope. The ship's telescopic rangefinders streamed directly into his optic implants, giving him a spliced view of both ships. Crosshairs appeared as his fingertips settled on the control pads, tingling briefly when the synapse contacts engaged the neuroreceptors. He locked onto the targets and the smartsystems did the rest, calculating the range and trajectory in nanoseconds, then adjusting the positioning of all thirty-six hull-mounted turrets to be in the perfect position.

"I've got them on scope, sir," Kedric said over the chatter from the other stations.

"Hold fire," Girbach said.

Kedric's scope lit up as his interface identified over fifty inbound projectiles. Each targeting box turned green as the SmartSystem established a weapons lock. "HV's incoming."

"Take them out, Mister Sonoda. Fire at will."

All Kedric had to do was push the button. One down. Six more went green and he fired without hesitation. Three shots missed, thrown off by laser scattering or some other diversionary tactic. The projectiles were coming in too fast. He set the turrets to fire on a pattern spread to try and take out as many as possible. A flickering of boxes vanished from the display, but not all of them.

"Brace for impact," Clydeman said. The ship rumbled and Kedric's scope went white.

"Damage Report," Girbach demanded.

Clydeman scrutinised his display. "No direct hits, Sir."

"Good. Throw everything we've got at them, Mister Sonoda."

Kedric flicked his view back to the scope. Now that the blinding light from the explosions had dissipated, he could see the attacking ships up close. They were an old blocky design with sharp angles and square edges. They were covered in black light-absorbing lamination, which barely contrasted against the star-speckled backdrop.

They were already too close for hyperbeams; Kedrick switched to the rail drivers and launched a spread across their arc. One slipped past, and within seconds it was close enough, he fired the electrothermal accelerators. Problem was, they weren't slowing to intercept, they were doing a pass by. The enemy closed the gap of ten thousand kiltrons in a matter of seconds, then they were heading away from the battle. It was the perfect time to strike.

The lock indicator on the two main targets went green. Before he could give the command, the ship rumbled violently. The scope went dark, and the screech of tearing metal deafened him. Inertia pulled him away from his seat, flinging him about like an invisible tornado, but the suspension fields held him in place.

When he looked around, the control room was in disarray. Fire suppression jets built into the floor and ceiling smothered eager flames, alerts blinked on every interface, and officers staggered back to their stations. Looking out the viewing portal, he could see a large egg-shaped pod jutting out of the hull. Insectile legs on the pod latched onto the ship's metal plating.

"We're being boarded," Clydeman said, ripping open a wall panel to expose a rack of handheld blasters. He took them out one by one and distributed them to Girbach and the other officers. The last one he tossed across the room and Kedric caught it with both hands. The charge indicator and sight appeared in his optic implants. He raised the weapon and the safety interlock switched to 'live fire'.

"Hold the bridge," Girbach ordered, pointing his weapon towards the port side entrance. He spoke into his link, "Security, get a team down to the hold and remove that Martian cargo."

A distorted voice replied, "Sir, we're being boarded, I need every hand available to—"

"They're here for the cargo, soldier. Get it off the ship. That's an order!"

"Understood, sir."

A tense silence fell over the room, except for muffled shouts beyond the control room doors.

"All this for some Martian cargo?" Kedric said. "It makes no sense."

Girbach snorted. "You don't use a battleship to move just any old cargo. Looks to me like the Martians have set us up."

The door snapped open and Kedric held his shots when the first people through were wearing blue and white, the UAE colours. Corpses. Behind them were grotesque abominations wearing body armour. They pushed the dead crew forwards, using them as meat shields. The Friendly Fire Inhibitor in his blaster wouldn't let him get a shot off. The mutants stood two metrons tall and looked like deformed 'roid junkies. He aimed high to satisfy the FFI and started shooting, but the shots ricocheted, leaving only a scorch on the mutant's warty hide. One invader bared pointed teeth at him, tossed its human shield aside and lunged across the room. The fist collided with his head like a boulder, then everything went black.

When he awoke, Kedric was lying on the floor, an invisible force bound him, pressing his arms to his chest. The room was filled with smoke, and the emergency lighting flashed red, but the fighting had stopped. The rest of the bridge crew were with him at the back of the room, bound in similar positions. All except for Girbach. The XO's headless corpse slumped in the command chair.

Four hulking mutants gathered around, talking to the Martian representative with the orange hair and a scar down his face, who had accompanied the exigent cargo. Kedric couldn't make out the words over the ringing in his ears, but the Martian pointed at him and one of the mutants approached.

Kedric groaned, struggling against the invisible binding. "You've taken the ship, got the cargo. What more do you want with us?"

The mutant sneered. "You will take us to *Altos-4*. Congratulations on your promotion, Captain."

Kedric didn't know how to react. He was expecting a prolonged and painful death at the hands of the mutants, not a field promotion. "Captain? Why me?"

The mutant grinned, exposing pointed teeth. "We executed the captain and executive officer. Our informant tells us you're the next in line."

"No, I mean, why do you need *me* to take you?"

"They're expecting this ship. You will fly right past their defenses and give us access to the cave of wonders."

The air on the command deck still smelled of burnt chemical smoke and it made Kedric cough. "Well, you can go fuck yourselves. We're loyal to the Colonies. You're going to have to kill every single one of us and learn how to fly this ship yourselves."

Kedric knew that the ship was next to useless without the command codes that he now inherited via the chain of command, but he would let the mutants work that out after he and his crew were dead.

The mutant lunged forward, seized Kedric by the throat and pinned him against the wall. "I know what you're trying to do, but we aren't going to kill you. We're just going to make you suffer." Kedric kicked his legs about, feeling the entire weight of his body hanging from his neck and wondering how his head was still attached. He gritted his teeth and stared defiantly back at the grotesque mutant. He could hardly breathe. The edges of his vision started to fade and he prepared to embrace death. Instead, the mutant released him. Kedric's feet touched the ground, his legs buckled and air rushed into his lungs. There he lay on the cold hard floor gasping for breath.

"Bring him to the hold," the mutant said.

Before Kedric could protest, he was heaved up over one of the mutant's shoulders and carried away like a disobedient child. "Put me down," he demanded. "If you're going to torture me in front of my crew, at least give me the dignity of walking there myself."

He couldn't see if there was a silent exchange between the mutants. No words were spoken, but they stopped and he was set back on his feet. The mutant who had been carrying him shoved him forwards and so he walked—hands still bound to his chest—through the empty corridors to the cargo hold.

The doors opened onto a steel walkway overlooking rows of containers mag-locked to the deck. They pushed him over the edge and a suspension field broke his fall, lowering him gently to the floor. The mutants followed, landing with a soft clank of their boots touching down on the metal plating.

The exigent cargo had already been opened to reveal a stasis chamber, a long cylindrical glass container with a mutant frozen inside. Tubes ran all over him, interlacing around his neck and vital organs. Though he wasn't grotesquely deformed like the others, the man inside simply looked ridiculously oversized and muscular. The cylinder was set upright, like a statue of some mythical deity casting judgement over them.

A mutant approached the control interface at the base of the stasis chamber and entered a command. A vial ejected from the side filled with crimson blood. It was locked it into an injector and handed it to another mutant.

Kedric started to back away. "What is this?"

A mutant grabbed him by the shoulders and tried to hold him still while the other approached with the injector, pointing its long menacing syringe in Kedric's face. With no way to run, all he could do to try and avoid the needle was to turn his head, but even that only delayed the inevitable.

"Stay still, unless you want to lose an eye," the mutant said.

He watched the needle approach slowly and enter the inside corner of his eye. It stung, but was not nearly as painful as he expected. Then pressure started building in his brain like a headache and his perception of reality started to waver. The room seemed to melt away and his heartbeat filled his ears like someone pounding on a drum. The deity in the chamber loomed over him, and he felt the presence of someone else in his mind.

Surrender to me and you will be rewarded with greatness.

"How are you doing this? You're frozen in stasis."

Not for long.

"Who are you?"

I am the next evolution of humanity. You will bend to my will and do my bidding.

"What if I refuse?"

Our bloods are now forever mingled. You can never be rid of me, until death.

Kedric tried to resist as the other presence relentlessly bombarded his thoughts. He had been trained to withstand torture and interrogation at the academy. Taught how to create barriers in his mind and to lock himself inside. This was nothing like his training. The thoughts seeped in like water through cracks in a cave wall.

"Get out of my head."

It's too late for that now.

Kedric realised the entity was wearing him down, and he fought harder, pushing away the thoughts of giving up, of not fighting any longer.

"Why are you doing this? You've already taken the ship."

Open your mind and I'll show you.

"I'll never let you in my—."

You don't really have a choice.

Kedric felt like the invisible barrier between their minds was melting. The blood was making its way into his brain, carrying with it the microscopic biological connection to a being that was no longer human.

What was the point of resisting? He was completely powerless to stop any of the events set in motion. He was just a cog in the machine, playing his part like everyone else. He was exhausted and fatigued. The sooner he gave in, the better it would be for him and his crew.

He needed to accept the situation and embrace his new master. His consciousness faded and vision dimmed until eventually there was nothing.

When the room came back, Kedric was lying on the floor, his arms still fastened across his chest. His head ached and he was drenched in sweat. He looked up at the empty stasis chamber. The floor was cold from the residual wisps of vapour that flowed out of the container. Kedric's heart began to race.

"I'm right here," the voice said in his head and out loud in unison. It hurt his brain.

He turned to see the supposed next evolution of humanity. Kedric's new master. He was tall and muscled, with skin almost as pale as his white hair. Dark patches around his bloodshot eyes indicated he hadn't slept for cycles. But there was also something inhuman about him. Something that Kedric couldn't quite figure out.

"Someone on the crew activated the comms array and sent a message," a mutant said.

Kedric instantly recalled the automated status feed.

"It wasn't the crew," his master said. "The ship sends out automated status updates to the fleet. We'll need to report back to the fleet commander and let him know we were able to destroy the threat."

The mutant in charge grinned. "How long until we get to *Altos-4*?"

Kedric tried to blink away the fog from his brain, tried not to think of the answer.

"Damage to the *Elysium* was trivial. Once the crew have repaired it, we will embark. Tell your soldiers to be ready in two hours." Kedric couldn't tell if he had spoken or if it had come from his master. The line that separated his consciousness from the other felt like it was getting thinner and thinner. He could barely tell which thoughts were his anymore.

The next evolution of humanity grinned at him and reality began to melt again. Kedric could sense himself slipping away. It felt like falling, even though he was vaguely aware of his legs still being firmly planted on the floor. The darkness felt like a release. It embraced him and he was at peace.

Free at last.

CHAPTER TWO
Call for help

*G*alaxy's cargo hold was illuminated only by a grid of surface lighting strips that spanned each relative floor, casting distinct colours across the containers. Raynor glanced at his wrist; the time appeared as soft glowing numbers. The loading access doors hummed as they retracted, and the gently pulsing yellow caution lights added to the sombre ambience. A gust of air swept in, bringing the smells of the Europa Orbital Space Docks with it. The burnt chemical stench of engines and machines contrasted sharply with the inodorous sterility of the internally filtered air. An external platform extended to meet the threshold with perfect precision and made a soft thud as it gently kissed the hull.

Raynor requested a connection on his Link. "Logistics, this is *Galaxy* on pad six, ready for the scheduled delivery. Please confirm?"

A monotone voice responded, "We're ready to receive cargo. Transfer the inventory schedule."

Raynor sent the requested files. As each container received an automatically allocated space in the warehouse, suspension fields picked them up and carried them out into the darkness. It was times like this when he wondered why humans still needed to be part of the equation. Perhaps it was a need to be in control. Maybe deep-seated trust issues. As dreary as it was, at least this was better than getting shot at.

While he waited for the cargo hold to empty, Raynor scrolled through the news feeds on his Link. He flicked past some stories about the instability of the Saturn Alliance in the Nexus and something about a new Lunar space station, but stopped on the headline 'UAEN BATTLESHIP ATTACKED BY OUTLAWS.'

His eyes flicked across the screen, looking for any key details, but he suspected the report was intentionally vague. The announcement was intended to scare people enough to justify the formation of the fleet without actually admitting weakness or incompetence. He was happy he was back to mundane deliveries and not in the midst of it.

"Everything's received and accounted for," the monotone voice said. "Please notify traffic control of your expected departure time."

"Yeah, will do. Thanks."

It had taken them two rotations to get to Europa for less than an hour in port. He thought about booking a transit pod to take him down to the surface. See the sights and take in the local culture. He could even ask Persephone to join him. Then he looked out at the empty platform and wondered about all of the things that could possibly go wrong. Every time he left the ship he seemed to attract trouble.

His Link chimed and an alert popped up with an encrypted message from Cliff, his Dispatch Supervisor. He ran their standard decryption sequence and the recorded message started.

Cliff looked panicked, his orange hair slicked back with grease or sweat. "Raynor, I need your help. I'm on the *UAEN Elysium* headed for *Altos-4*." He looked around nervously, then back at the Link. "Mutants have taken over the ship and have forced the crew into servitude. You have to convince Mars, or the UAE, to send ships. There's one more thing. It's about Reen—" The message cut out, leaving Raynor staring slack-jawed at the frozen image.

Rob was in his workshop on the engineering deck when Raynor walked in. The ship's engineer was tinkering with Abel—a thin layer of synthetic skin stretched over a carbon fibre frame, tensile cables instead of muscles, machine oil instead of blood.

Raynor nodded towards the android. "How's the patient?"

Abel opened one eye, his head slowly rotating to meet Raynor's gaze.

"When Abel died, I took a snapshot of his brain. Storing it as raw data is easy, but converting it into a virtual structure to simulate a working brain is complicated. An organic brain has billions of neurons and synapses firing together in almost unfathomable combinations to create thoughts, driven by memories and external stimulations. That is pretty much impossible to replicate with current technological limitations."

Raynor raised an eyebrow.

"Still broken," Rob said. He looked up and scowled at Raynor. "You never come here to enquire about my work, what's the matter?"

"Remember those geared up outlaws we encountered recently?"

"You mean the advanced fighters we found on Enceladus?"

"Yeah, the ones packed in *Altos-4* branded containers."

"What about them?"

"I think I have a way to find out how they got them."

Rob crossed his arms. "What happened to wanting just one delivery run without getting shot at?"

Raynor shook his head pensively. "It was nice while it lasted. I received this message from Cliff."

He played the message back and watched Rob's expression change from annoyance, to concern, to intrigue.

Rob stroked his beard. "It's about Reen ..."

"What do you think that means?"

"Well, Mars didn't know what to do with him. Makes sense that they'd send him to *Altos-4*. The real question is, how did the mutants get involved and what part is Cliff playing?"

Raynor scowled. "Cliff? You think he is involved somehow? He was terrified of the mutants, I can't imagine him going to these lengths to work with them."

"He would if he could gain from it somehow," Rob said. "Maybe he wanted to be the hero that foiled a mutant threat and thought he was safe aboard a UAEN destroyer."

"When it backfired on him," Raynor agreed, "he sent us a call for help. I don't think Cliff would have ever intended for us to actually go to the authorities, either."

"Then why did he say that?"

"He knows us better than that. It's not like he had a lot of other options. But this could be a good opportunity for us."

Rob nodded. "The recent outlaw attacks, the Artifact, and even Reen. It all leads back to *Altos-4*. If we can get in there and find a way to directly access their data core … "

Raynor rubbed his temples, feeling the early onset of a stress headache. "Alright, so what's our next move?"

Rob entered some commands on his workstation and a partial map of the solar system appeared above it. "What was Cliff's location when he sent this?"

Raynor flicked the file from his Link to the interface on the workstation and Rob manipulated the 3-dimensional map. It now included green dots for the *Elysium*, *Altos-4* and *Galaxy* connected with curved lines estimating their trajectories towards the belt.

"This message was sent nearly an hour ago," Rob said. "Assuming the *Elysium* is still heading for *Altos-4*, we're not going to reach them first."

"So is this still a rescue mission or a salvage operation?"

"We won't know for sure until we get there. Regardless, *Altos-4*'s nexus isn't run by a standard SmartSystem. You have to assume that everything they have is far more advanced than anything we've encountered before. We're going to need Lisa's help if we want to pull this off."

Raynor closed his eyes and ran his hand through his hair. "I know she appears to be playing our game, but Lisa is still an Observer working for Swift. At some point she is going to use all of what she has learned against us."

Rob nodded. "This is worth the risk. Let's make sure we're prepared for it when she does turn on us and we may just stand a chance."

Raynor took the mag-lift down to the crew deck and entered the infirmary unannounced. Appel was busy at her workstation. It was hard to visit this place without remembering the violence of Swift's incursion when the Prime came to drag Reen away for conducting illegal genetic research on himself. The damage was gone, but not the scars.

Appel caught him gazing at one of the diagnostic pads. "Raynor," she said with a pleasant smile. "Something I can do for you?"

Raynor forced a smile. "I've got a mild stress headache. Came by to get a disc."

Appel tapped a command into her Link and gestured for him to sit on a metal stool next to her work bench. He removed his jacket first and slipped onto the padded cushion. A machine on the wall ejected a med-disc that Appel collected before standing behind Raynor. She massaged his shoulders with the familiarity of two people who worked and lived together in a relatively confined space. "You're tense," she said.

"I'm always tense."

She pressed the disc into the skin on his neck and applied force with her thumb. When she released he felt the warmth of the chemical reaction as it dissolved into his skin. "Not *this* tense. What's on your mind?"

Raynor spun around on the stool to look at her. "I wanted to ask you about Reen."

Appel inhaled sharply, and stood up a little straighter. "Reen?"

"You knew what he was doing. What he was trying to achieve."

"No!" She looked away. "I mean, I was helping him with his condition, but I had no idea—"

"Appel," Raynor said, putting both hands on her shoulders. "This isn't an interrogation. I just need to know what happened. What state of mind he might be in if he were to come out of stasis."

Her eyes widened. "Are we going to recover him?"

Raynor nodded. "I've received some information that indicates he is being transferred to a facility called *Altos-4*. There may be an opportunity for us to poke around so I want to be prepared for whatever he has become."

"Um … all our research was confiscated by Swift's techs. I have no way of knowing what actually happened or what went wrong."

"What do you remember about the procedure?"

Appel walked around the bench and sat back in her chair. "Reen had a genetic condition called Idiopathic Polygenic Necrosis. It basically meant his body was decaying at a cellular level. The procedure we designed was meant to essentially re-write his DNA to exclude the IPN strands."

"Hence the secrecy," Raynor said.

"Yes. We thought the less the rest of you knew, the better. We were going against some significant regulations. I know these limitations exist because of the mutants. But this was different."

"How so?"

She took a deep breath and then looked Raynor in the eyes. "He was my friend."

Raynor ran his fingers through his hair. "Okay, so you figured out how to cure him."

Appel nodded. "Everything was set up. We encoded the RNA into a sequence of med-discs that would trigger and accelerate the changes. It should have returned him to full health, but …"

"But it didn't," Raynor suggested.

"No, it did. It far surpassed all of my expectations. I was long overdue for a sleep shift and we both had agreed that it would be wiser to be fully rested before beginning the procedure. When I got back to the infirmary, Reen was already there completing the final preparations. It was only after the effects started to manifest that I realised he had made changes to the encoding. I don't believe this was an accident. This was exactly what he wanted."

"So he used you without any regard for the consequences. Now we're all caught up in the crossfire."

"Wouldn't be an issue if you were all law-abiding citizens," Appel said sharply.

Raynor grimaced, then stood and paced around the infirmary, headache forgotten. "Say it had worked exactly how he intended. Swift hadn't interrupted, and you had finished the sequence. What do you suppose he would have become?"

"From what I observed, the muscular development would have made him three, maybe four times stronger. Rapid cell regeneration would make him heal much faster. He was able to fight off a team of elites in full combat armour. But those were just the cosmetic changes. His bio-monitor was showing signs of significant internal changes to his organs and even his brain. If I had to guess, he was attempting to increase his cognitive abilities as well as his physical ones."

"What do you think he would have done with that kind of power?"

"Red has a copy of his standard psych evaluation. There were no indications of megalomania, narcissistic, or sociopathic tendencies. Of course, that doesn't mean he didn't develop those later. I thought I knew him. I thought he was a desperate man trying to find a cure. Maybe he just got greedy. What would you do if you had access to that sort of power?"

Raynor reached for the Artifact in his pocket. The one he couldn't bring himself to part with. The one he had killed for. "If the procedure warped his mind, there is no way of knowing if he is even the same person. Is that what you're saying?"

"I don't think we can really know what to expect. If you do happen to encounter him again, I would suggest using extreme caution."

"You must have had something in place in case it all went wrong?"

Appel looked off in the distance, deep in thought. "There was a fallback option. In the event his body didn't respond well to the treatment, I had a med-disc encoded with his original DNA. I managed to slip it in my pocket before the Prime kicked in the door."

Raynor rubbed his chin. "I'm going to need you to come with us on this one, and bring the disc."

DATAFILE
Altos-4 Sentry

NODE 1

The *Altos-4* Sentry System consists of autonomous humanoid mechs designed to defend the station in the event of a breach or outbreak from any of the projects under development in the laboratories.

NODE 2

Each unit is composed of a metal alloy armoured frame containing an electroactive polymer actuator system controlled by an organically grown replica of a human brain. While each unit has a self-contained Smart System to drive it, the Sentries are controlled centrally via the *Altos-4* Systems Processor Core (SPC).

Each one is armed with mounted weapons, including: retractable shoulder-braced missile launchers, high-velocity smart round cannons on each forearm, and a close combat Tectanium sword with a magnetically sharpened zero-point blade. There are several failsafe measures implemented such as compartmentalised systems within the frame to ensure it can continue to operate under extreme circumstances.

NODE 5

Each unit contains a sophisticated synthetic brain architecture capable of complex thought and a synaptic feedback system. However, due to the intentionally limited scope of their programming, they are considered to be non-sentient. Thereby excluding them from having any rights or privileges under 'The Nexus Peace Treaty: Node 4 - Human Rights'.

CHAPTER THREE
Stipulation

Lisa's awareness cycled between deep sleep and awake, one of the many advantages of the cybernetic hardware within her brain. Her eyes shot open to the chime from Raynor pressing the query command on the door to her habitat.

Dawn broke in her virtual wallpaper. The holographic walls slowly brightened, and she deactivated the suspension field holding her weightless in the middle of the spherical room. She turned a section of the wall into a mirrored surface and checked her appearance. The black body suit she had slept in would be perfectly suitable.

Another chime sounded as Raynor pressed the query again. A mental command from her allowed him to enter. "What is it?"

Raynor hesitated. "Sorry to disturb you." He narrowed his eyes. "Is something the matter?"

"No," she said defensively. "What do you want?"

"Just to speak with you," Raynor replied. "Can I come in?"

"Fine," she said hesitantly, then stepped back from the entranceway. With a discreet hand motion, she activated a mid-level suspension field and sat.

Raynor sank into the field and took a deep breath. "We've been through a lot recently. I feel like we haven't really had a chance to debrief after Enceladus."

Lisa had kept to herself since the events on Luume. Raynor had lied to her and put her in direct danger. How could she ever believe anything he said? "Why don't you get to the point? What do you want from me?"

Raynor frowned, he opened his mouth to speak but stopped himself, then tried again. "A unique opportunity has presented itself."

She studied his expression, looking for any sign of deception, but his eyes revealed nothing. "For what?"

"We have a chance to uncover the truth about what is really going on within the Colonies."

"There is nothing going on—"

"Don't give me that," Raynor said. "One sub' ago, the outlaws were a myth. Since you came on board, we've encountered them on three separate occasions. Each time, they have been operating right under the Colonies' noses, with technology they shouldn't possess."

She tried to think of an argument but came up empty.

"*Altos-4* were the ones who provided the Fighter technology on Luume," he continued. "We need to find out why."

"*Altos-4?*"

"It is a highly advanced research facility. Very few people even know about it. It's their tech that we saw on Luume. I suspect that they may be responsible for all of these outlaw attacks."

"How do you know all this?"

"I've been there before," Raynor said with a devious smile. "If we can get access to the *Altos-4* database, we'll be able to know for certain. All we need you to do is go in there and hack into it. You know, undetected."

Lisa crossed her arms. She felt like she was being used. Again.

Raynor held out a data crystal. "Take this. All you have to do is connect it to the primary data-node and it will give Red a direct uplink."

"Oh no!" Lisa said. She pushed the crystal back at Raynor. "I'm not getting involved."

"All you ever do is get involved. Last time, your intervention saved an entire colony from being wiped out. This is even bigger!"

"What you're talking about is madness! Infiltrating a secure node in familiar territory is one thing, but a facility that is so secret that I haven't even heard of it? It's going to be far more dangerous."

"So, you're scared."

"Yes! And you should be, too. If they catch you, there is nothing to stop them from killing you to protect their secrets. I'm the last cyborg left in existence, if they catch me, who knows what they'll do?"

Raynor leaned forward. He placed the data crystal in her palm and enclosed his hands around hers.

"You don't have to do this alone."

For a moment, Lisa indulged the simple comfort of human contact, then pulled her hands back from his and looked away. It was her job to find out the truth. The main reason for her still being here. But she was tired of yielding the initiative to him.

"I'm sorry, Raynor. But I can't help you." Lisa looked at him directly, working hard to keep her composure. "You're getting involved with things that are much bigger than we can handle. Let me get Swift to look into it."

Raynor stood up and turned to leave. "If Swift learns about it, *Altos-4* will disappear, and we'll never learn the truth." He paused and looked back at her. "That data crystal has everything we know on *Altos-4*, Reen, and the outlaw encounters we've had. At least take a look at it and see if you can find us a way in. We're doing this with or without you."

Lisa took the data crystal but remained silent. She couldn't even bring herself to look at Raynor as he showed himself out. After she heard the door reseal, she closed her eyes and explored the data.

Millions of glowing symbols drifted around Lisa in an endless black void, each one representing a datafile. The whole construct shifted and shimmered in response to the ceaseless data calls from reality. Many were connected by thin white lines, but her mind struggled to navigate the ever-changing digital landscape. She focused on Reen, the medical practitioner assigned to *Galaxy*, the one who had triggered this whole mess. Files related to Reen began to order themselves in front of her. There were thousands of them, many of which she had seen already. The problem was that the profile she had constructed from the data didn't match up with what she knew about him. It didn't make sense that a low-profile infirmary tech would suddenly unlock the human genetic code and start making improvements on himself. Her brain was enhanced by a neural network that was capable of processing every last bit of data, allowing her to look for patterns and get the big picture. But she couldn't see it.

Why don't you try looking at things differently?

Red's voice echoed through the virtual construct. The ripples of his words changed the structure of her surroundings. She was now floating in water, looking up at a starry sky. Red reached for her hand and pulled her up.

Where are we? Lisa thought.

Still in the same place, Red answered. *You can use your mind to render the information in a format that makes it easier to process. This is just one example.*

Lisa had seen Red plenty of times, lurking around in the background of the interface displays that appeared in every room of the ship. This was the first time she had ever been so close to him. He looked more real here in this construct. He was taller than she was, with piercing green eyes and an amused smile.

Why don't you give it a try, he suggested.

Lisa searched her mind, trying to think of something visual. She had the strange sensation of finally being allowed back into a locked room after having forgotten everything about it. This skill was something the Colonies had taken away from her.

A vision came to her of an ancient library, with rows upon rows of bound paper books. The image rendered, forming the room around them. They stood at a crossroad of aisles with lofty ceilings and stairs that led up to a balcony containing more rows of books. Red looked around and his smile broadened.

Lisa put her hands on her hips. *How is this meant to help me? It could take me cycles to read all these books. And I still don't know where to start!*

Ahhh, but now you get the concept. Look closer at the headings.

Lisa looked up. Each aisle was labelled: 'Medical reports', 'Procurement', 'Calibration Schedule'. None was of any interest to her. She noticed an aisle called 'Research'. She walked down the rows of books, running her hand across them as she read the titles. Each one came with flashes of information, previewing what was inside. She stopped at one called 'Genetic Resequencing' and picked it up.

Again, the surroundings changed. She was in the infirmary on *Galaxy*. Red was still with her, watching quietly. Reen was in a suspension field, and Appel stood before him holding a folder of med-discs. They were frozen in that moment, unmoving, unless Lisa willed it.

Now you see, Red said. *When you put things in the correct perspective, the relevant information finds you.*

Lisa nodded. It was all starting to come back to her now. She examined the datafiles on the holographic interfaces surrounding the lab. She didn't have to read them to consume the information, she simply became aware of the content.

He was sick, she said, then looked at Red.

The Interactive Persona smiled, but there was sadness in his eyes. *Reen was going to die. This was the only way he could be saved. But it wasn't just about that.*

No, she agreed. *This research is … it would have changed everything.*

She played back the whole scene, filling in the missing pieces with her own recollection of the events. Swift tore open the door, the Prime rushed in, Sharn and Ellam fought with the monster until Swift finally managed to subdue him through force.

So why were they moving him to a top secret facility?

Red queued up the datafiles and rendered them into a white room full of blue doors. The floor was reflective, but the walls and ceilings seemed to expand into an abyss. *This is everything we know about Altos-4. You may remember, this is where we were supposed to deliver the exigent cargo, back when you first came aboard.*

Lisa walked past one of the blue doors, brushing its wooden surface with her fingertips. A brass handle, cold to the touch, twisted gently to let her in. On the other side was a room full of tiny screens cataloguing all of their past visits. She stood and watched briefly, but none of it seemed useful. Some of the images contained great walls of stone, indicating the complex was somewhere underground. The hallways were clean and spacious. Dark figures stood in alcoves set into the walls that looked like armoured guards.

The door closed with a soft click and she walked past two more, fingers reading each one like invisible brail. The third one caught her attention. On the other side was a room with racks full of data nodes. Millions of lights flickered like stars in the sky. She opened some of the nodes: a digital handshake with their security systems granting permission to approach, a more invasive scan of al l *Galaxy's* systems, instructions to delete all of their logs—which Red clearly ignored. Lisa turned to face the Interactive Persona.

Red, did someone program you to override security requests?

His expression didn't change, he just stood in the void, staring back at her. Red's pleasant smile returned and he said, *Raynor asked me to ignore the request and retain the information.*

But why?

Red shrugged, still smiling. He didn't offer any further explanation. It irritated Lisa how well he emulated human expressions.

She turned her attention back to the handshake and regular pings from the security system, hoping there was something in the code she could exploit. Buried somewhere deep in the inventory exchange was the thread she was looking for. To anyone else it would have looked like an indexing check, but to her eyes, it may as well have been a handwritten note. A message in a tube. A call for help. It was so subtle that she couldn't derive any further information other than it had been created by one of her own kind.

It seemed impossible, but her heart fluttered with a glimmer of hope. Somewhere, buried deep within the code of *Altos-4*, there was a cyborg held captive, and they had somehow managed to implant this distress call into the security protocols.

Lisa tried to suppress her emotional response. Distantly, she felt the prickle of sweat on her real-world skin, then the ripple of the suspension field swiping it away. Her mind shifted back into that body. Eyes taking in the virtual backdrop of her habitat, golden rays radiating through tall trees.

She opened a connection to Raynor.

"Hey," he said with a friendly smile. "Did you find anything we can use?"

"Yes, there may be an opportunity to exploit their code and send a packet ahead of us. But there is something else."

Raynor raised an eyebrow.

"I changed my mind about helping you," Lisa said.

Raynor's smile widened. "That's gr—"

"On one condition," she said. "I want the Star device."

"What do you want with it?"

"I need some assurance that I can escape if things get out of hand. If you want my help, that's my price. You can have it back when we're done."

Raynor scowled and looked away, took a deep breath and released it slowly. He held up the small silver sphere to the camera on his Link. "This thing is ancient technology. It's irreplaceable. It's also exactly the sort of thing that *Altos-4* is collecting. Don't lose it!"

Lisa nodded. "I have one more thing to do, then I'll meet you in the control room to go through the plan."

Lisa waded through long grass in a dense green forest. It wasn't quite like any environment they had on Mars or any of the other colonies for that matter. But realism wasn't all that important here. The aroma of flowers on the soft breeze and the simulation of a larger sun on her face, the sound of birds chirping around her. They were all meant to optimise the levels of dopamine, oxytocin, serotonin, and endorphins released into the brain. It was a 'happy place'.

She found Abel sitting by an open wood fire in front of a compact log cabin. They were nestled in a gully surrounded by tall mountains. He was almost unrecognisable from his android incarnation. He was tall and thick-bodied, but not fat; the typical Martian stereotype. He had black hair and a beard speckled with white. He gazed at the fire, so engrossed by the dancing flames that he didn't look up as she approached.

"Do I know you?" he asked in a deep sombre voice.

"Yes. We've met before … after your accident, that is. I'm Lisa."

Finally, he shifted his perch on the tree stump and looked up to regard her with soft eyes. "Do you still think I'm an abomination?"

"No," Lisa said. Then, with a shrug, "I'm sorry I said that. I didn't really mean you. I meant what Rob had done to you was hideous."

Abel shook his head. "What are you doing here?"

"We need your help. The crew are boarding *Altos-4* and we need you to go ahead to check if it's safe.

"What?" Abel looked down at his chest then back up at her. "I have a barely functional body, what am I going to do?"

"I'm not asking you to help in a home-made human costume," Lisa said, then a holographic projection appeared next to her, of a menacing armoured guard. "This is state-of-the-art security tech from *Altos-4.*"

Abel raised one arm and his masculine body morphed into an armoured mech-suit. Only his head stayed the same. He frowned, the lines on his forehead creased, making him look even older. "Why me? Can't Red do it?"

"Red wasn't designed to operate these sentinels. Sure, he could learn, but it would take time. Your brain patterns have had more experience with a similar model. You've driven a body like this before."

Abel examined his hands. "This construct is the only place I've been able to think clearly and reflect since *it* happened."

"I'm sorry—"

"Don't be. It is what it is. We all have to die sometime."

The tree stump was unnaturally flat and large enough for two, so Lisa sat down next to him. "But you're not dead. You're still here."

"Is this what passes for an afterlife now?" Abel waved his mechanical hand at the impossibly blue sky. "I was promised an eternity of sweet nothingness … I feel ripped off."

She didn't have time for this, but she needed Abel to comply willingly. She looked up at him. Watched the fire dancing in his eyes.

"What was it like? Dying, I mean."

Abel poked the fire and the embers leapt up like a thousand fireflies. "I don't really remember. I imagine the trauma of it all probably didn't convert very well when Rob did … you know, scanned my mind and digitised my thoughts. Everything seemed like a dream, but now, in this place, I almost feel … human."

"This place isn't real. You'll exist here as an echo for the rest of your life, if that's what you want to call it. This operation is risky, but I'm offering you a potential second chance at a physical existence in a high-tech prosthetic or a better death than what you had the first time."

Abel scratched his face. "And what if I don't want to do this?"

"The crew are going regardless. If you don't, then there is a good chance they will all die."

Abel nodded gravely and paused as if in thought. "Fine. I will help."

DATAFILE
Altos-4

NODE 1

Altos-4 (named from the Latin word Altus, meaning 'high, deep, noble or profound') is a private research facility buried deep within the Asteroid 'GX-78082' in the Mars-Jupiter Belt. It was designed to facilitate covert scientific experimentation and research in a secure, isolated environment that evades external scrutiny and bypasses ethical constraints imposed by the Nexus.

NODE 2

A section of the asteroid's interior was excavated and reinforced with radiation-resistant shielding, creating a robust and self-contained environment to house the complex.

The facility consists of: sixteen state-of-the-art laboratories, central operations, six storage warehouses, occupant Habitats and recreational areas, two ship-docks, eight Gen-12 AST Fusion Reactor Cores, hydro-plant, and Sanctuary.

NODE 3

Multidisciplinary teams drive breakthroughs at the cutting edge of scientific innovation, supported by engineers, technicians, and security personnel. With dedicated laboratories focused on biotechnology, genetic engineering, nanotechnology, and robotics.

NODE 4

Altos-4 was constructed in C1053 and has been operational for over 46 Cycles. In that time it has seen various refits and upgrades.

CHAPTER FOUR

Contact

Asteroid GX-78082 filled the interface as they approached. Black shadows stretched across the rocky surface as it twisted slowly in the harsh sunlight. As far as celestial objects went, this one was quite plain. It looked like every other object in the belt: brutally carved stone shaped by countless collisions.

Diputs hovered weightlessly in the centre of the control room, held by a suspension field, surrounded by glowing charts and graphs from the holo interfaces. Rob paced back and forth, stopping occasionally to stroke his beard or inspect some details on the wall projection. Jake and Appel sat in moulded chairs at the back of the room, playing a 3D holographic game. It appeared to involve a glowing dot bouncing off a grid of cards that changed colour when either of the players touched them.

The mag-lift doors opened, casting a warm light across the room. Raynor turned to acknowledge Lisa, who paused to look out the front viewscreen as she entered.

Lisa frowned. "Is that it?"

"The space station is deep under the surface," Rob said, pointing to a small dark spot in the centre. "That's where we make our entrance."

"Are they not going to make contact?" Appel asked.

"They would have seen us coming a long time ago," Diputs said. "The fact that they aren't talking to us and haven't turned us to space dust doesn't bode well. It's possible we're already too late."

Rob shook his head. "Some of the most advanced tech in the Colonies defending that asteroid. There's no way they would have gone down that easily."

"There is supposed to be an automated system that verifies our approach," Lisa said. "If they were attacked, it's possible the whole station went dark. My estimation is they are either in lockdown, or there is nothing left to defend."

Everyone exchanged nervous glances, but they stayed on track. The rock on the screen grew larger in their scope.

Raynor crossed his arms. "How does that affect our entrance strategy?"

"Won't know until we get closer," Lisa said. "Once we're in range, Red will have access to their automated docking control system. I can use that thread to send in our advanced boarding party."

"Good enough for me," Diputs agreed. "Taking us in."

The ship descended into a ravine. It narrowed, deepened; the black opening of a cave appeared ahead. *Galaxy* was tiny in comparison to the jagged mouth luring them into darkness. The scanners mapped the cave as they went further inside, and overlaid the enhanced image over the blackness. The walls were encrusted with craggy rocks that looked almost like rows of teeth, as if the asteroid were a monster about to swallow them alive.

The tunnel twisted and turned, continuing to close in around them. At some points, it felt too narrow for the ship to pass. In reality, it was just an illusion of scale. The ship passed through a gap between two rock faces that opened up into an expansive cavern. Red highlighted the defensive turrets jutting out from the rock, almost indistinguishable to the naked eye. They could have easily shredded the ship's hull, but they were all deathly still.

On the far side of the cavern was a metal structure built into the rock face—the lack of guide lights and darkened windows made for an unwelcome reception. Three ships were docked at extendable bridges, reaching out from the lower levels.

One of the ships was the *UAEN Elysium*. Its hull had long scars and scorch marks where it had taken damage. The other two ships were unregistered but looked like salvaged cruisers with some heavy modifications. Sheets of thicker hull plating had been welded on, and a long cannon jutted out, capable of launching something the size of a transit pod.

A cluster of sleek black probes with thin insect-like appendages appeared to be making repairs to the battleship.

"Red, what are those things?" Diputs asked.

"They are fabrication drones. I wasn't able to query them using any standard calls. They're probably programmed for automated repairs."

"They don't look like any robotoids I've ever seen before," Diputs said.

"At least they aren't shooting at us," Lisa conceded.

Red appeared on the holo, giving the illusion he was standing in the room with them. "I've established a connection with their auto-docking system, so they aren't ghosting us. None of their other systems are responding, though."

Lisa nodded. "Can you send the package?"

"I have a clear path to the security grid. Package delivered. This is strange, though. There is still a strong barrier stopping me from accessing any of the other core systems. It's almost as if someone wants us to get inside."

"That's what I was hoping for," Lisa said.

Raynor raised an eyebrow. "Care to share with the rest of the class?"

"Just a hunch. I'll let you know if it turns out I'm right."

"It worked," Red said. "Abel has booted the sentry's OS and is sending us a visual feed from inside the station."

"*This* was your plan?" Raynor asked.

"Let's see it, then," Rob said.

The front viewscreen changed to a live feed of the sentry's optical input. Pulsing red emergency lights gave them glimpses of chaos and destruction. Smashed glass and debris from explosions littered the floors. A haze of smoke from flickering flames obstructed their view.

Galaxy had been one of the only ships entrusted with the charter to deliver cargo to the secret laboratory. Raynor remembered the glossy white surfaces and calm blue lighting, glass windows separating the corridors from the work areas. Now, metal blast shields replaced windows, and the charred walls in the dim light looked like something out of a horror sim.

"Still want to go inside?" Lisa asked.

"Not really." Raynor took a deep breath. "Going to anyway."

Abel, now firmly in control of the sentry, looked at his new hands and tested each finger individually.

"What's it like?" Rob asked.

"No offence," Abel said in a slightly robotic voice. "It's a lot better than the one you made."

"To be fair, they probably had teams of engineers working on it for cycles," Rob said. "Tell you what, if nobody over there objects, you can keep it."

Able moved carefully through the debris of the ruined structures. "It looks like whoever attacked this place was using some pretty heavy munitions." He cycled through filters as he explored, then stopped on one that looked like a heatmap crossed with motion and vibration detection. A reddish orange blob moved nearby. "I think I've got company."

Raynor tensed. "Hostile?"

"Not shooting at me. It appears to be a survivor."

The docking seal indicator went green and the doors opened into a transition chamber, which scanned them with a narrow beam of light. Raynor looked around at the rest of the boarding party, gauging their readiness. Lisa carried a small hand blaster, while Persephone had an assault rifle. Rob, Jake and Appel were unarmed. All wore spacesuits. An interface on the wall showed that the pressure and oxygen on the other side were at safe levels, so he tapped the controls and the door slid open.

Blood splatter stained the floor, streaked down the corridor where a body had been dragged away. Raynor retracted his helmet and immediately smelled the pungent mix of charred flesh and explosive residue. "Let's get to Abel and the survivor first, then try to establish a secure perimeter."

Glass crunched under Raynor's boots as he cautiously approached one of the sentries. He waved his hand in front of its faceplate, then clicked his fingers. "Hey, anyone home?"

The armoured sentry stood motionless.

"I really don't think we should be here," Jake said.

Lisa went straight for the nearest interface, ignoring the carnage around her. Everything was quiet but for the crackling of a distant fire and the hiss of air filters trying to extract the smoke. "There is no response from their interactive persona. The whole system appears to be in some sort of safety mode."

"What can you get us?" Rob asked.

"I've got the floorplans. Abel is in a lab not far from here. I can't tell which areas are still intact, though."

"What about their security systems?"

"I don't have access," Lisa said, pointing down the main corridor. "Abel is this way. Follow me."

As they got deeper into the labs, the destruction was more spread out. Doors were smashed or pried open, flames danced untamed across workstations. In some corridors, they found dismembered corpses, white coats stained with blood. In others, they found the broken remains of sentries strewn across the floor. Regardless of the death and destruction, there were no signs of any slain mutants.

Through the smoke and darkness, a silhouette appeared ahead. Unmoving, the figure stood in the middle of the corridor, arms crossed.

Lisa raised her blaster. "Abel?"

"Welcome to *Altos-4*," he said in a modulated voice.

Raynor put his hand on the android's shoulder. "Ready to do some killing, big guy?"

Abel's head turned to acknowledge him. "I thought this was a rescue mission."

Behind Abel was a man slumped against a wall, eyes glimmering in the torchlight. He raised an arm against the sudden brightness.

Appel pushed past Raynor and placed her medical tool kit next to the survivor. "Can you tell me your name?"

"I'm Salem Mills," he said uncertainly.

"I'm going to give you something for the pain," Appel said. "Lisa, can you give me a hand to stop the bleeding?"

Lisa knelt down on the other side of Salem, took a skin repair patch out of the kit and applied it to his arm. "Can you tell us what happened here?"

"Their clearance checked out, we were expecting the cargo." Salem winced at the pain. "But it was all a trap. All this technology and we were undone by a Trojan Horse."

"A what?"

"Ancient philosophy. We took the cargo, thinking it was secure. The specimen was supposed to be in stasis … but those mad creets let him out."

Lisa's jaw dropped. "The mutants?"

Salem nodded gravely. "They were too strong. We were powerless to stop them. I don't remember anything after that."

"You're lucky," Appel said. "It looks like your injuries are limited to a few lacerations and a mild concussion."

"What were you working on here?" Rob asked.

"There are many things that …" Salem trailed off, his eyes fixated on Lisa. "Ahh, you have a cyborg. I'd heard rumours about you …"

"Rumours?" Lisa asked. "Are there other cyborgs here? Tell me!"

Salem's gaze wandered the ground, his jaw clenched. For a moment, he looked confused. "I … don't …"

Lisa grabbed him by the front of his coat and growled through gritted teeth, "I need to know!"

"I don't know anything," Salem whimpered.

Appel placed her hand on Lisa's shoulder. The cyborg slowly relinquished her grip, but she didn't break eye contact.

"As much as I'd like to see where this goes, we need to keep moving," Raynor insisted. "The mutants will be around here somewhere. Once we find a defensible position, we can venture out and try to get to the datacore. Maybe you'll find your answers there."

"The datacore is heavily shielded," Salem said. "We're better off going back to your ship. I don't think there would be any other survivors."

Raynor pulled the scientist to his feet. "We're not going back to the ship until we get what we came for. No offence, but I just don't trust you to give us the truth of the situation."

"Hey, look at this," Persephone said as she slipped through one of the wrecked doors.

Raynor followed Lisa through the door. His eyes widened at the sight of row after row of glass canisters filled with a bubbling grey fluid. This lab was less damaged than the others. Raynor didn't recognise any of the shapes inside until getting closer and inspecting them. A clawed hand grasped emptiness in one vessel, a heart pulsed softly in another. Eyeballs watching them attached only to brain tissue was the worst of all. None of the body parts appeared to be completely human, but rather, some sort of animal-human hybrid.

"What are these atrocities?" Lisa said, shining her wristlight around the tanks.

Salem took a deep breath. "Our work here is the cutting edge of biochemistry. Sometimes, you have to break a few rules to make progress."

Towards the end of the lab, the specimens looked more like complete bodies. Some of them even looked close to human.

Lisa stood frozen in the doorway to the next room. "My kind were slaughtered for the threat we posed to humanity. Yet, all the while you have been creating your own monsters."

"The Nexus is afraid of progress," Salem said bitterly. "But there are some who see the necessity in pushing evolution to its limits. Every failed attempt is a lesson."

Raynor shone his light in Salem's face. "You should probably stop now. You do *not* want to piss her off."

Lisa was no longer listening. Raynor followed her gaze. In the centre of the room was a cylinder, larger than all of the others. The creature inside had a breathing mask over its face. It was at least two and a half metrons tall, with four arms and three long spiked tails. Red hair floated around its head, disturbed by the air bubbles pushing out of the mask.

Whatever it was, was still very much alive. It reminded him of Reen, but this thing was bigger and more evolved. The changes didn't appear to be haphazard or accidental, as was the case with most mutants. This creature looked specifically designed to be a predator.

"This isn't one of ours," Salem said cautiously.

"We need to go," Jake said. "We should leave as quickly as possible and destroy this place."

Raynor shook his head. "I don't want to be around when that thing wakes up either, but we can't leave now. Rob, is there anything you can do to keep that thing contained?"

Rob approached the interface at the base of the tube and flicked through the different datafiles. "To be honest, biology isn't exactly my area of expertise. Whatever they're doing, I have no way to tell what it is or when it's supposed to be finished. One thing's pretty clear, though. We've found our dispatch supervisor. This *thing* is Cliff Burton."

DATAFILE
Fabricators

NODE 1

Fabricators are autonomous spider-like robotoids designed for advanced construction and repair operations. Their primary function is to create and manipulate materials at the molecular level, utilising a combination of Alchemic Manifestors and Suspension Fields. Their sleek hexapod design, featuring six thin retractable multi-tool appendages, enables exceptional agility and precision.

NODE 2

The Fabricators were developed by a team of elite technicians under the direction of Principle Researcher Salem Mills at the *Altos-4* Science Institute Robotics Division. Following an intensive research and design period spanning several sub-cycles, Mills and his team reached key technological breakthroughs in Atomic Manipulation. The end result was a versatile machine capable of organic and inorganic manufacturing in a fully-automated capacity.

CHAPTER FIVE
Absolutism - C1096 S01 R09

C lifford Eddison Burton looked up at the clear Martian sky. It was a fine day, and warm for the current part of the cycle. His focus wasn't really on the blue bubble of artificial atmosphere that extended around the planet, but rather the impossibly tall buildings reaching up around him. He looked down at the entrance, braced against the vertigo, and blinked to check the time index on his Link. 10:23:05 glowed briefly in the corner of his eye and faded away. He had just enough time to ride the mag-lift up to the ninety seventh floor for his assignment review. His fate would soon be determined by the outcome of this meeting.

Inside the spacious lobby, the interactive persona greeted him with a generic smile. "Welcome to ORA Tower. Your role reassignment consultation has been scheduled for ten thirty in room ninety-seven twenty-eight. If there is anything else I can help you with please let me know."

Cliff proceeded to the ring of mag-lift tubes and stepped onto the first available platform. He grabbed the handrail and the lift gently pushed him up through the transparent tube, whizzing past each floor.

ORA was the acronym for Organic Resource Allocation. Leave it to the Colonies to consider all of humanity in terms of biological value. He had studied political science for the last three cycles and would now be assigned to a position, possibly for the rest of his life, based on the needs of the Mars Colony. He knew he hadn't scored high enough to qualify for a role in The Nexus, and his family didn't have the right connections. But he was still hoping to get a preparatory role in the Mid-Council or Executive Committee.

The lift came to a stop at the ninety-seventh floor and the safety glass slid open. It was another lobby of sorts, with corporate blue and white carpet, warm lighting, comfortable seating and green plants filling the blank spaces. He went straight to room twenty-eight, and the door opened for him in anticipation. An older gentleman in a professional-looking cream suit stood to greet him. "Mr Burton, my name is Seraan Barker."

"Thanks for meeting with me, Mr Barker. I'd like to dispute my assignment as a Dispatch Supervisor."

Seraan nodded towards the chair. "Please, sit."

Once they were both seated, Seraan brought up a series of datafiles on his interface. "You have a prejudice about where you're placed?"

"My primary area of study was infrastructure, so I was really hoping for a position at either a Council or Committee level."

"That's a little more modest than I was expecting. Political Science graduates usually want to be a Peacekeeper, and think they'd be the perfect candidate. Your goals are still ambitious nonetheless. Based on your various evaluations and the current opportunities available, I think you are well suited for your appointment at the Mars Logistics Entity."

Cliff's heart sank. He could feel his stomach twisting, a flush of anger rising in the place of his dying ambitions. He tried to keep his voice calm and even. "But a Dispatch Supervisor? It isn't even a political role."

"Listen, kid. You studied politics, you know how the system works. We just don't need any more counsellors or planners at the moment. What we *do* need is people to manage our vast network of resource distribution and storage. If you embrace the position and do the work, you could very well end up as an MLE Executive."

Cliff nearly laughed out loud. But the reality of the situation was no laughing matter. "Is there any higher level I can appeal?"

"There is, but you need a compelling reason why you should be considered for reassignment. There would need to be other placements that you would be suitable for, and—"

"*Are* there any other positions I would be suitable for?"

Seraan sighed and flicked through a datafile. "Political Science skill sets don't really lend themselves to a lot of other fields. Believe me, this is the best opportunity you're going to get."

Two subs later, Cliff was standing in the main hangar of Distribution Centre Thirteen watching the transports take off and land. The best part of this utter disappointment of a job placement was the impressive sight of enormous vessels touching down with pinpoint accuracy, and listening to the humming of their engines as they defied gravity. He was sitting on a hover platform stacked high with containers waiting to be loaded, when a smaller and newer looking freighter landed right in front of him, sending out a gust of air.

The landing ramp extended, opening up the ship's cargo hold, and a man with short scruffy hair and a serious expression strolled down the ramp to greet him.

"Hey, are you Cliff?" he said.

"Yeah. Raynor, is it?"

Raynor nodded and ran his fingers through his hair—which didn't make it stick up any less. "So you're our new Dispatch Supervisor. How are you finding it?"

"I studied Political Science for three cycles so that I can stand around here making sure the automated systems put the right cargo on the right ship. How do you find this line of work?"

Raynor cracked a grin. "I did a tour in the MSCF during the war. So far I haven't been ordered to kill anyone since I transferred to Logistics."

"No shit. You were in the Space Combat Fleet? What was your rank?"

"That's not important." Raynor rubbed his chin. "I get the impression you're not exactly thrilled with your placement."

Cliff hesitated, wondering if there was some sort of test or trap in the question. But this guy wasn't a politician, he was just another pawn who was assigned a meaningless role, destined to move cargo for the rest of his pointless life. "You could say that, sure. But what choice do I have?"

Raynor shrugged. "Look at the bright side. Being a politician comes with a lot of responsibility and even more scrutiny. But at our level, no one really cares what we get up to as long as these containers reach their destination. If you had your own agenda, there is quite a lot that you could accomplish here."

Cliff narrowed his eyes. "Accomplish? Like what?"

Raynor took his Link out of his pocket and held it up for Cliff to see. "This little piece of software is a passive signal encoder. I'm running it right now. Means if anyone were trying to listen into our conversation, they would have no idea what we were talking about." Raynor held the device out for Cliff to accept the file transfer. Cliff took out his own Link and held it underneath Raynor's. "Best part is, it hides in your OS and is pretty much undetectable if anyone were to run a diagnostic."

"Thanks," Cliff said. "But why?"

"I need a favour. Nothing too serious. I just need you to arrange for us to take on some extra cargo from time to time, give us some leeway with our schedule; stuff like that."

"What's in it for me?"

"Maybe, you get to enjoy taking a few risks and defying the system that put you here."

"Shit," Cliff said. "Shit, shit, shit."

A wave of nausea hit him like a punch in the gut. His heart was racing. He thumbed through a tiny container of black market med-discs which he always kept on him and administered something to calm his nerves. A rush of endorphins hit him and he took a deep breath, encouraging his heart rate to return to normal.

He looked back at the stasis tube containing Reen and knew exactly why the mutants had sent him here. If Reen was able to successfully make enhancements at a genetic level to living subjects, then it would transform the course of humanity forever. Exactly the reason it was forbidden by The Nexus.

Paranoia made him check that the encryption program on his Link was still running, then synced the container's transponder so he could keep tabs on it if it got relocated. He locked the hatch behind him and climbed back onto the hover platform.

As the platform zipped through the warehouse, Cliff pinged Ziak an encrypted call request. After a few seconds, Ziak accepted the connection. The mutant looked like a demon. Off-coloured skin, deformed bone structure, fang-like teeth. Cliff had to remember not to react.

"That container," Cliff said. "It's going to be near impossible to move it. Even harder to make it disappear. There will be people keeping a close eye on it."

"It's true we will need to bide our time," Ziak said thoughtfully. "There is a covert research station hidden in an asteroid in the belt—"

"Yeah I know the one. What about it?"

"We're certain the Martians will send the container there to study the specimen inside. When they do, you will pick the ship and accompany the cargo to its destination. Once we have what we want, you will get your immortality."

"And what if I refuse?"

"Then you won't live very long at all."

Cliff nodded. "I'll let you know when it's time to move." He ended the connection.

He took another deep breath. The calming agents in the med-disc he had absorbed left him feeling a little lightheaded and foggy. But just under the surface, a storm of anxiety loomed. He made another connection request, this time to Raynor.

It took a while for him to answer. "Cliff, how are things?"

From his surroundings, it looked like Raynor was in some place public.

"Are you in a secure location?" Cliff asked.

"Not really. We're on *M1*. But this is an encrypted Link, and no one's in earshot, besides Diputs. What's the matter?"

"They threatened to kill me …"

Cliff heard the collective gasp from the captured crew as the mutant forced Kedric to his knees and brought up a blood-filled syringe. The look of defiance on the commanding officer's face was replaced by calm acceptance. The needle was driven in with fast precision, and the room was filled with silent anticipation. Kedric's body tensed, then it was all over and he stood up like nothing had happened.

"Damage to the *Elysium* was trivial," Reen and Kedric said in unison. "Once the crew have repaired it, we will embark. Tell your soldiers to be ready in two hours."

Ziak nodded and started herding the crew out of the hold. Cliff was startled when a mutant he didn't recognise grabbed him by the arm and started pulling him towards Reen.

Cliff tried to resist. "What are you doing?"

"We want to have a little chat about what you know."

He felt his pulse racing again. Reen watched them approach with a neutral expression. One of the other mutants was pressing med-discs into his own bare chest. Cliff looked around to see if anyone was holding an injector gun filled with blood.

"Relax," Reen said. "You are a friend to our kind. Without you, I wouldn't be standing here."

"It's true then?" Cliff asked. "Have you mastered the skill of genetic manipulation? Can you prevent death?"

"I'm living proof." Reen spread his arms. "I was on the verge of death, and now I have transformed into something far greater than my original form."

"Then you can do the same to me?"

Of course. You will be the first of a new, better version of humanity. Together we will transcend war and dogma. We will push the boundaries of biological existence until we become the living embodiment of divinity.

"How are you in my head?"

Reen grinned. "So, your friends have the Artifact."

"Raynor never admitted to it. But I know when he is lying. I was there when he was being questioned and I have no doubt that he has it."

"Then we must ensure he comes to *Altos-4.*"

When Cliff went back to his cabin, he recorded a call for help and sent it to Raynor. He dropped just enough information to pique Raynor's interest, corrupted the data a little to make it look like the message cut out unexpectedly, then sent it and destroyed his Link. The act in itself was like destroying an invisible shackle that the Colonies had chained him with all this time. It was regrettable that he had to betray Raynor's trust like this, but it couldn't be helped. He was so close to greatness now that all he had to do was reach out and seize it.

When they arrived on *Altos-4,* he waited behind. He was no fighter. The mutant who came back for him was covered in blood and missing an arm. The broken and charred interior of the facility told more of the story. The crew of the Elysium had been the vanguard for the assault, forced into combat so they could be used as meat shields. Dead bodies lined the path to his transformation, all of them human.

It seemed like a good idea when Cliff agreed to help the mutants. They just wanted to push the bounds of evolution without persecution, and in return, they would give him artificial longevity, perhaps even immortality. But now, walking through their trail of destruction, he was beginning to wonder if he was going to get more than he had bargained for.

Reen and the other mutants waited for him in a laboratory. It looked like they had hooked up an external power generator to some kind of incubation chamber.

"I was under the impression you could just give me a couple of med-discs," Cliff said nervously.

"This is a whole new treatment," Reen said. "My procedure was crude and rushed. Yours will be a complete transformation."

"Hang on a second. That's not what I agreed to," Cliff said, backing away. "I just want to live forever in my current body." He bumped into a mutant standing behind him. All eyes were on him. The positioning of the other mutants made it quite clear there was nowhere else to go. No escape.

This was his fate.

As the clear tube closed around him and filled with some kind of bubbling liquid, Cliff went into a psychedelic trance. Re-living the events of his life leading to this moment. Reen's voice in his head was maddening. It was all Raynor's fault for putting him in this situation in the first place. The Colonies made him into a resource, Raynor made him a criminal, now what would Reen make him?

CHAPTER SIX
Metamorphosis

Raynor ran his fingers through his hair. "Are you sure that's Cliff?"

"I don't suppose this info display has any reason to mislead us," Rob said.

"Can you reverse it?"

Rob shrugged. "Don't look at me."

"Why would you want to reverse it?" Salem pushed past Rob to get to the interface. "This is incredible."

"That's our dispatch supervisor," Raynor said. "They've turned him into a monster."

"But look at these changes. Increased body mass, extra limbs. Look how his tail splits into three, each one tipped with some sort of hardened spike. Your dispatch supervisor has been made into a weapon. Our research was largely based on trying to expedite natural evolution. These enhancements have been expertly crafted. The application possibilities for this are endless."

"Wait a second," Jake said. "Reen cures himself of a terminal genetic disease and gets detained, frozen, and prosecuted as a dangerous criminal. But here, he can transform another human into some sort of enhanced predator and it's commendable?"

Raynor raised an eyebrow. "The Nexus opposes all forms of genetic modification, life saving or otherwise, and they use stories about mutants to justify their position. But this isn't Nexus. This is something else."

He watched Salem take a copy of the data from the interface.

The scientist nodded. "Could you imagine if everyone could make themselves stronger, smarter, and omnipotent? The power struggle that would ensue would be catastrophic. In the wrong hands, then yes, this technology could have disastrous consequences."

Raynor realised he was fidgeting with his blaster and put it back in its holster. "What would that make this place, huh? The right hands?"

"This facility isn't just for research," Salem said. "We are the gatekeepers of all kinds of technology that could upset the delicate balance of power in the Colonies. It is our sacred duty to not only pursue all knowledge, but to keep it safe."

Raynor gestured at the damaged parts of the room. "Seems to me like you haven't done a very good job then."

Salem scowled. "You have no idea how great the impact of our work has been."

"Like the weapons on Luume?" Jake asked. "Or a space station crashing into Lunar?"

"More like the mutants," Appel said from the back of the room. Everyone turned to look at her. "It's no mere coincidence that they have come back here. You created them and sent them out into the system."

"Humanity needs an enemy," Salem said. "Be it the outlaws, mutants, or even cyborgs. It's how the Colonies stay united and at peace."

"So the Nexus are the ones behind all of these atrocities?" Persephone asked, without taking her eyes off Cliff. "The Cyborg War, the destruction of *M1*, all of the outlaw attacks. It's all just a ruse?"

Salem shook his head. "The Nexus are nothing but bureaucrats. Do you really believe they are the ones calling the shots?" The scientist's expression changed, his eyes widened. "Where did your cyborg go?"

Everyone glanced around the room. Even Raynor had been too preoccupied with the discovery of Cliff to notice Lisa slip away. He tried sending a connection request. "I've got no signal. I don't suppose you know how to get any of the internal systems back online?"

Salem shook his head. "There is no time for that. We need to go back to your ship."

"We're not leaving Lisa behind," Raynor said, surprised at his own words. Though she had the Star, she could still get into trouble. "Persephone and I will go look for her. The rest of you should stay here with Abel and make sure our dispatch supervisor doesn't escape his tube."

"I'm coming with you," Salem said.

Raynor glared at him.

"I think actually we should all go," Persephone said, still looking down her scope at Cliff.

A mechanical whine emanated from the stasis chamber. Amber lights flashed around its base. A stream of bubbles rose through the tube, and the fluid level began to drop as cracks danced across the glass.

Jake backed away slowly. "Do you think he is going to be happy to see us?"

"Let's not wait around to find out," Raynor said. Turning to leave, he saw the doors to the lab close and the locking indicator strip turned red. Through the reinforced window, he could see Salem standing on the other side. Raynor ran to the door and pounded against it with his fist. "What are you doing? Let us out of here!"

Salem activated the comms. "I'm so sorry, but I very much want to see what this weapon is capable of before I begin the purge. At least now you'll be dying in the name of science."

Raynor spun around. "Abel, we need a way out."

"This entire room is sealed off. I don't think I'm going to be able to break us out."

Appel, Jake and Rob took cover behind a row of workstations. Persephone still held her blaster rifle trained on Cliff, and Abel armed his wrist-mounted cannons.

The glass tube splintered and crashed to the floor, leaving Cliff standing naked in the centre of the room. He stretched his new limbs and flexed.

"Cliff, we came to get you," Raynor said, his back against the lab door.

Cliff looked at him, eyes focusing like a target lock.

"Are you still in there, buddy?"

"You …" Cliff growled. "This is all your fault."

Cliff leapt towards Raynor, crossed half the lab in two bounds, then veered sideways as Persephone hit him with a burst from her blaster. Cliff changed direction, now trained on Persephone. Abel had already anticipated, and moved to intercept. He pushed Persephone aside and swung his mechanical fist at the monster. Metal and flesh connected, the impact sending Cliff tumbling to the ground. He wasn't there long. Whipping himself up, he sneered at Abel and the two squared off.

Cliff whirled, lashing out with his three bladed tails. Abel dodged one, grabbed another, but the third pierced his armour. He responded with a blade of his own, extending out of his arm, which he used to slice clean through the flesh. Cliff roared in agony and rage. The gap that opened between them allowed Abel to activate his rapid-fire cannons. The sound of thousands of tiny projectiles being fired in just under five seconds was almost deafening.

It should have been enough to tear anything, man or machine, to shreds. But Cliff still stood, braced against the onslaught. Everyone watched anxiously to see if he would drop to the floor. But still he stood, arms covering his face, breathing slowly. Blood filled the holes in his flesh and sealed around the wounds almost instantly.

Cliff lowered his arms, looked at Abel, and began to laugh. The lights flickered out, and the droning of the oxygen recyclers died.

Everything was dark and still as Raynor began to drift into the air. He fumbled for a handhold in the wall to steady himself. If the power was out, this was their chance to escape.

CHAPTER SEVEN
Alerya

Lisa scanned the corridor for structural integrity. It wasn't secure, but also unlikely to imminently collapse on her. She decided not to linger nonetheless, hurried along by the metal creaking under the stress of the rock constricting it. The irregularity and unfamiliarity of the sounds made them impossible to ignore.

It was a risk separating from the others, but the discovery of Cliff allowed her to slip away unnoticed by the *Altos-4* scientist. She had her own reasons for coming on this mission. It took ten minutes to navigate the creaking corridors to the data core. The door looked like any other. Completely unremarkable except for the lack of any visible damage. She queried the interface and the door hissed open to reveal what could only be described as a mutant graveyard.

Bodies lay strewn across the white floor, their deformed faces twisted in agony. She had found the invading mutants. Blood caked under their eyes, and white foam gathered around their mouths like they had been poisoned. They had carved through *Altos-4*'s defences, slaying any humans and machines in their path. But here, something had found their weakness and wiped them out.

The door closed behind her and the white light panels lining the walls, floor, and ceiling turned red. She could sense something evaluating her and waited for an incoming connection, a ping, or some sort of contact point. In an instant, the pressure changed. All of the oxygen cycled out of the room. She tasted the acrid bite of chlorine, and quickly switched to her internal rebreathing system. Her body was capable of scrubbing the carbon dioxide from her last breath and recirculating the same air for a prolonged period of time, but it wouldn't last forever.

Lisa looked around at the datacore. *You're going to have to do better than that if you want to stop me.*

As if in response, she was hit by a wave of pressure that almost knocked her off her feet. It was blasting her away from the control interface in the centre of the room. She fought against the sonic wave, pushing against the pressure and forcing herself forwards one step at a time.

She reached out and placed her hand flat on the interface. In a flash, her surroundings changed. Lisa could see the internal components of the security system, which her mind translated into a maze.

She raced through the enclosed passage, winding her way through the twisting corridor of black reflective surfaces, illuminated only by the dull blue glow her avatar emitted. The passages seemed endless, branching and forking, adding to the structure's complexity. A couple of times, she reached a dead end and spun around, doubling back to try a different path. Each intersection and hub looked almost identical and she could no longer tell which direction she was meant to be going. Instead of letting it get to her, she relaxed. This wasn't a real maze. The memory of Red's instructions resonated, she could control this, it was just another construct. Instead of following the maze's path, she ran at the wall and the smooth black surfaces turned to brittle shards as she smashed through them.

Lisa opened her eyes and the pressure was gone, the room returned to its default white light. Her interaction with the security protocol lasted only a fraction of a second in real-time.

Easier than expected.

She took the data crystal Raynor had given her and placed it on the surface. The display lit up as it connected and began authenticating the uplink. While it processed, she decided to do some digging of her own. Planting both hands firmly on the interface, she closed her eyes and plunged her awareness inside.

Lisa's vision faltered and darkened. When she regained focus, she was in a wide corridor that looked oddly familiar. She tried to move the walls with her mind, but found she had no control over this construct. She followed it into a circular room, a ring of glass wrapped around the floor and ceiling. A processor matrix in the shape of a tree rose from the lower level, reaching its glowing branches into the ceiling above. This was a virtual construct of her first home; the facility where she was created and grown.

It made no sense for her to be here. But who else could be controlling this environment? And why *this* place?

Her childhood was not like a normal person's. She was the product of science and evolution. The 'next stage of humanity'.

Every phase of her development was planned and executed with precision in a place that looked just like this one. But it no longer existed in physical reality. It had been destroyed during the Cyborg War when humanity had come to the conclusion that the next evolution meant the end of the line for them. Lisa had been extracted before her maturation and used against her kin.

She stepped into a room that had not existed in the original building. A beautiful stone fountain drew her attention, representing a complex array of processing nodes. She approached the edge and looked into the water to see a whirling matrix of holographic symbols spinning beneath the surface.

She reached into the water. The chill numbed her hand. She flinched and gritted her teeth as the raw data surged up her arm, through her body and into her brain. Images and files flooded her mind. In spite of the regulations, the scientists of *Altos-4* worked tirelessly, tinkering with the genome, growing, splicing, enhancing.

People who failed rehabilitation were sent here. Their heads sliced open, examined, and prodded. They were changed, moulded, destroyed. Then the process was repeated, time and time again. Many of the abominations turned on their creators, some succeeded and escaped.

But it wasn't all torture and abuse. Other departments collected and studied technology of unknown origin, coveted by their influential benefactors. The question of who or what created them eluding even the all knowing elite.

In that single touch, a profound awareness dawned within her, unravelling the true nature of *Altos-4*. The scattered fragments coalescing, the revelation of an enigmatic organisation that stood apart from the Colonies, above even the Nexus. They weren't only interested in the next evolution of humanity. They were trying to create omnipotence in physical form. Her eyes widened with disbelief.

She withdrew her hand, hesitating a moment. She had to have more. But before she could, someone called out to her.

Help me!

The agonised voice echoed through the room and hit her with a wave of fear and despair.

Who's there?

She ran out of the room and towards the central processing tree. One of the doors on her right caught her attention. She tried to open it and a window appeared, just big enough for her to look through. Inside was a little girl she didn't recognise, restrained in a suspension field. The girl thrashed about, desperately trying to break free. Once she noticed Lisa, she screamed. The deafening pitch caused Lisa to cover her ears. Everything around her started to break apart, the construct destabilising and shattering around them.

The nightmare doesn't end! The girl screamed. *The Darkness is here …*

Lisa looked around. The room shook and rumbled. The lights were flickering out around her, plunging them into pitch-black. But there was something else, the feeling of being watched, dark clouds reaching out from the edges of the room. She had to get out.

Like waking from a bad dream, Lisa forced herself back into her body. The panels in the interface room were flashing red in time with a low-pitched undulating alarm. She focused on the interface in front of her. The data transfer was only four percent completed. She brought up a section monitoring all of the systems to see what was happening. The readouts showed coolant temperatures, current, voltages, bandwidth, beta waves, and … a pulse? These weren't the readouts of a datacore, this display looked like human vital signs.

No—Not human …

The construct of her home and the girl inside wasn't just a simulation. It was someone hiding from a reality far too horrific to put into words. She entered the commands to open the biocontainment chamber and a metal sphere lowered from the ceiling. It opened with a puff of steam, and Lisa stepped back in breathless disgust at the sight in front of her: suspended in a nest of cables and tubes was the ravaged body of a cyborg.

She had found the prisoner.

Her arms and legs were gone, severed at elbow and knee. Fibre optic data lines sprouted from the stumps. Metal tubes and glowing cables violated her flesh. Her face twitched in agony.

Lisa felt ill, hit with wave after wave of anger, revulsion and despair. She reached out and touched the pale white face of the cyborg, no longer the little girl from the construct. Just another resource to be exploited.

Lisa opened her mind to form a connection between them and instantly felt her pain. It was a suffering that couldn't be quashed by the concoction of intravenous drugs they fed her to keep her docile and compliant. There was still a small part of her, trapped in the depths of insanity, longing for a life that she had been deprived of. All that was left to her was never-ending abuse of her mind and body. They had turned her into a living and breathing data processor.

Alerya. That was her name. The name that was stolen from her, like everything else. They had taken everything away from her, so Lisa would take everything from them. First, she had to overcome the immediate threat. The Darkness was still plaguing the cyborg; a virus pumping through the critical systems, spreading out like a black cloud, corrupting everything in its path.

Lisa knew what she had to do.

She drew back and took a sharp breath, almost a gasp. Her eyes shot open, head pounding like she'd been struck. Somehow, she managed to remain standing. She paused for a moment and waited for the pain to subside.

The drone of the oxygen filtration systems ceased, the lights failed. *Altos-4* was shutting down. "What are you doing?"

"The Darkness is here," Alerya whispered.

"What is the Darkness?" Lisa asked. "Why are you shutting everything off?"

Alerya, the beating heart and brain of the station, looked back at her in the dim emergency lighting. "It's the only way to stop him."

"Who? Cliff?"

A tear ran down Alerya's pale cheek. "No. There is one more powerful. He wants to take over. You can't let him."

"I won't. Tell me what to do."

"You got my message," Alerya said wistfully.

"Yes. I saw the clues you left for me in the inventory exchange data packet. I came to save you."

"I didn't invite you here to save me. I want you to free me."

Lisa shook her head, because she knew why Alerya was asking. Physically, they had mutilated Alerya's body, but the psychological damage was worse. She didn't know how anyone could ever recover from such abuse.

Tears stung her eyes. She had finally found another like her and now she had to play executioner, again. "I can't. I already betrayed our kind once. They're all dead because of me." Lisa choked on the w ords.

"No … there are others."

"Where?"

"Seek them out, and you will see."

Alerya's eyes rolled back in her head. She was already too far gone. Lisa pulled at the cables connecting the cyborg to *Altos-4*. There were so many, but eventually she had removed enough that she could lower Alerya's body to the floor.

Lisa hesitated, then gently caressed Alerya's face. "I'm so sorry," she whispered. Her hand found the life support cable that was the last thread keeping the cyborg alive and gently pulled it out.

Alerya's eyes closed as the last spark of life left her and Lisa wept.

One of the cables still dangling in front of her was the main data line. It was thick and black with a sharp needle point. Lisa's sorrow quickly turned to anger. She grabbed the cable and jabbed it into the soft flesh behind her ear. Her receivers screamed at the foreign invasion. The edges of her vision flickered and blurred, random numbers and images overlaid with no logic or pattern. Her implants quickly meshed with the station's systems, sensor feeds finding receptors, data streams filling buffers.

The vault of immense knowledge cracked open, spilling its secrets like a hull breach. It's contents, vast enough that if every human who ever lived was given a share, it would take them a century to read it all. Traditional storage transfers wouldn't hold it all, and the process would be too slow. The only option was to use a technique called Genetic Data Transposition. The process involved storing the massive amounts of encoded data in the cells of her own brain. To speed it up, she located three more of the main cables and plugged them in. But there was something else in the expansive matrix of neurons and nano-processors, something that Lisa couldn't quite comprehend.

The presence that Alerya called the Darkness had been attacking *Altos-4,* infecting it like a virus. She could feel it, like a song stuck in her head. It invaded her mind, flowing around, over, through her counter-intrusion protocols. This was something else. Neither she nor the autonomous programs were able to classify it. In her mind she threw together a containment array and locked herself inside. It wasn't perfect but it would hold the Darkness at bay, for now.

She looked up, saw the nightmare forms of dozens of robotoids emerge from the walls and ceiling to scuttle towards her. With a blinding flash an ion torch flared from the belly of a robotoid, she couldn't describe the heat that ran across her with excruciating intensity. Almost so hot it felt cold. She let out a scream as the robotoids forced her down and began to connect her to the rig that previously held Alerya. Other bots began to rip holes in Lisa's clothes and skin. They attached wires and cables as she thrashed and fought against them.

Lisa struggled to reach her blaster, but it came loose with a click, then she started firing wildly. One of the robotoids fell to the ground in a mess of sparks and high-pitched noises. She managed to take out five more before the spiders removed the weapon from her grasp. She looked down to see the cables extruding from her skin, connected to all her essential cybernetic components. Lisa meant to free Alerya, not replace her.

The containment array holding back the Darkness began to buckle, and now it wasn't just her mind at stake but the whole of *Altos-4*.

The construct changed and she was back in her old home. The complex where she had been raised. Only now she was the one trapped here. A door appeared, opening in front of her and a dark haze swept through, forming the silhouette of a person. Someone she recognised. The Darkness grinned as his features sharpened. He looked younger than the last time she had seen him. No longer deformed like a mutant.

Thank you for your assistance, Reen said. *I didn't think I was going to be able to get past Alerya's defences. But now, I am in control.*

DATAFILE

Altos-4 Systems Processor Core (SPC)

NODE 1

The Systems Processor Core (SPC) is the primary component of the complex Node array that runs the control systems for *Altos-4*.

NODE 2

Smart systems are comprised of a sophisticated set of programmable directives designed to automate and optimise complex operations. While effective in managing routine tasks, these systems proved inadequate for analysing the intricate research requirements of the facility, necessitating a more advanced solution.

NODE 3

After a comprehensive evaluation and review process conducted by a specialised data analyst team, an organic solution was proposed that would revolutionise the computing capabilities of the facility.

On the advice of the Principle Solutions Designer, approved by the Operations Coordinator, three prisoners were transferred from ███████ to the facility to undergo compatibility testing. Only one of the units passed.

NODE 4

- Name: *Alerya* ███████ ID: L2411████████

- Gender: *Female* DOB: ███ ███ ███

- Generation: ████████

- Genetic Sample: 10002342426654/1000523110921

- Note: This unit was by far the most stable. Despite the trauma caused by ████ ███████ ████, a routine biochemical stabiliser has proven excellent ongoing results.

CHAPTER EIGHT
Preponderance

The emergency lights interrupted the darkness of the lab with their dull glow. Raynor caught glimpses of the genetically enhanced monster and mechanoid sentry, who were facing off in combat.

Cliff whipped his tails at Abel, the blades glancing off the hardened armour. Abel tried deflecting the blows to get in close, his feet mag-locked to the floor while Cliff used the lack of gravity to leap around the room.

Raynor turned his attention back to the exit. The door was standard low pressure internal. He felt about at eye level, found a catch and toggled it, thankful for the ubiquity of Martian engineering. Once the lock was open, Raynor pried the doors open just enough to slip through.

Cliff grabbed Abel by both arms, placed a foot on the android's chest and pulled. The metal creaked as it began to give way. Abel strained as he tried to pull his arms back. With a loud crunch, one arm came loose and was flung across the lab. Raynor's stomach dropped. This might be over before it had even begun. His blaster would be next to useless against the mutant, and he didn't want to draw attention to the open door. He gestured to the others to make their way over to him.

One by one, the rest of the crew escaped the lab while Cliff and Abel fought. But while Cliff seemed to be able to regenerate quickly, the sentry was amassing damage.

"What about Abel?" Rob asked.

"We need to get out of here," Raynor said. "When Cliff is done tearing that mechanical body apart he is coming for us. Want to be around when that happens?"

Raynor slipped through the doorway, and fell to the ground as the gravity returned. The lights powered back up, and the door swiftly slammed shut. He scrambled to his feet and peered through the window. Cliff was pounding on the glass, trying to get out. Cracks started to appear in the reinforced window.

Behind Cliff, Raynor glimpsed a red glow. Abel was on the ground, legs shattered, clutching at his stomach. Something in the centre of his sentry body was overheating.

"He is overloading his power cell," Rob said. "Not sure if this lab will contain the explosion."

There was a crackle as Raynor's link picked up a transmission from inside the lab. Abel's voice reached through the static. "Thank you for sticking with me, I will always—"

The detonation shattered the already cracked windows. Explosive containment doors snapped closed, trapping the blast.

The sound was deafening, and the shockwave knocked everyone down. Raynor's ears were still ringing as he used a workbench to pull himself back to his feet. He looked around the room. Everyone was still alive. Rob worked quickly on an interface to retract the heavy containment shield. The doors to the main lab were twisted and deformed. Beyond them, the lab was gone. Now just a hole in the rock, charred black and made smooth from the force of the explosion. There was no sign of either Cliff or Abel.

Appel had her medical kit out and was applying a skin patch to Persephone's forehead.

Rob was staring blank faced at the wreckage from the blast.

"Are you okay?" Raynor asked.

Rob shook his head. "I tried hard to keep him alive. I wanted to make it right."

"He died long ago, my friend." Raynor placed a hand on Rob's shoulder. "Neither situation was your fault. You did your best."

"So what do we do now?" Jake asked.

"Reen is still here somewhere," Appel said.

"Lisa is still here, too," Raynor added. "And I bet Salem will be going to the data core to try and protect whatever secrets they have been hiding here. That's where we need to go."

"Aww, how sweet! Here I was thinking you didn't care about me," Lisa said through the station comms, her voice echoing through the labs and corridors.

Everyone looked around.

"Lisa? Where are you?" Raynor said.

"I made it to the data core … found the other cyborg. Now I've taken her place."

"Can you get out? Salem tried to trap us in with Cliff. We lost track of him."

"I'm not alone in here. Reen is connected somehow, he has most of the systems under his control."

"What if we split up?" Persephone asked. "Some of us could go after Salem, the rest can go and find Reen."

Raynor combed his hair with his fingers. "I don't think we should split up."

"I've located Salem," Lisa said. "It looks like he is heading towards the reactor. If he gets there—"

"Shit," Raynor said. "Forget Salem, we should get out of here. Lisa, do you still have the Star?"

"What?" Rob exclaimed.

"Yes," Lisa said. "But I haven't finished copying the *Altos-4* data. You need to stall Salem to give me more time."

Rob raised his hand in the air. "Hold up a moment, can we just talk about why Lisa has the Star? That device is an incredibly rare piece of ancient technology!"

Raynor shrugged. "You wanted her help. That was the price. Besides, she's going to give it back."

"Am I?" Lisa said sweetly.

"Time's escaping, people," Persephone said. "Are we going after Salem or not?"

Raynor hadn't heard from Lisa for quite some time, he wondered if it meant that Reen had cut her off, or if she was just preoccupied with stopping him from taking over. Regardless, all of the security checkpoints were unlocked, allowing them to simply stroll in.

The Reactor complex was at the very heart of the installation. There was no damage from the mutant attack here, and it was eerily devoid of station staff. Large windows overlooked the miniature sun, contained in a gyroscope of spinning rings and suspension fields. It was like the one on *Galaxy*, only much larger. Salem stood atop a walkway above the reactor. Raynor pointed his blaster at the scientist. "Step away from the controls, Salem."

"You're too late," he yelled. "I've already disengaged the safety protocols. It's only a matter of time before the regulators fail and the reaction mass begins to rapidly expand. We should get back to your ship now."

Persephone ran up the stairs to the walkway. "We're not going anywhere. So you'd better fix whatever you've done here."

Salem grinned. He stood only metrons away, arms raised, palms open. "You defeated the monster. You are worthy." He slowly reached for a silver pin on his collar and flicked it towards Raynor. Raynor caught it one-handed, passed his blaster to Jake, and inspected the circular engravings that looked almost like an eye.

"I am a member of an organisation called the Illuminis," Salem said. "It's a collective of all the influential people in the Colonies. Together, *we* control the Colonies. We control everything!"

Raynor's eyes narrowed, trying to make sense of it all. "Why are you telling us this?"

"Because I can't let this facility fall to the hands of the mutants. It must be destroyed."

"You would destroy all of the work you've done here?" Persephone asked.

"And destroy all the evidence," Jake said. "You've been crashing space stations, supplying weapons to revolutionary outlaws, all to keep the colonies distracted while you created abominations to try and replace us.”

“You see it,” Salem said. “The bigger picture. You came here for answers and I can give them to you. As agents of the Illuminis you will be privy to the grand master plan. This complex alone doesn’t matter. There are others.”

“So what?” Raynor said. “We take you with us and you let us join your little club? Just like that?”

“If you help me, I will have you all inducted as agents of the Illuminis. You will have more power and freedom than anyone in the Colonies.”

Raynor looked up at the report of a blaster discharging and saw the scientist fall against the railing. He turned just in time to see Jake fire again, an intense focus on his face. The blaster cracked twice more, Salem fell back over the railing, plummeting into the glowing sun. With a short eruption he sizzled and was no more.

“Jake! What the fuck?” Raynor said.

Persephone and Appel protested in unison. Rob kept his judgement to himself.

Jake was trembling. He didn’t lower the blaster. “If there really is some elite ruling class, they aren’t just going to let us join because we know their secrets. We can’t just let them cover all this up and start again.”

Raynor suppressed a grin and wondered if he was perhaps becoming a bad influence on Jake. “Yeah, I didn’t trust him either.” He turned the silver pin in his hands and a data transfer alert appeared on his Link. The pin contained a data crystal.

DATAFILE
Illuminis Induction

Congratulations!

You've been accepted into the ancient society of The Illuminis. You are about to learn *the truth*.

--//DATAFILE CORRUPTED//--

CHAPTER NINE
Transition

Lisa reached out with her awareness. Past the suspension fields, past the construct, past the darkness. The *Altos-4* nexus was vast, and Reen was trying to trap her psychologically. She opened her mind and felt the walls of the construct rattle. She summoned Reen by visualising him.

Reen grinned. *Perhaps I underestimated you.*

Get out, Lisa said in a low, threatening tone. As she did the walls exploded into millions of shards and Reen's silhouette dissolved back into smoke.

The construct changed around her. She was running down a hallway with lavish red carpet, cream walls, and evenly spaced chandeliers hanging from a high ceiling. She stopped at the door to the sentry control systems and turned the golden handle, but it was locked. Lisa tried kicking the door, but it didn't budge. Chandeliers faded and vanished as the black fog crept after her. She kept moving, trying more doors on her way. They were either locked or she opened them to find Reen's fog had already crept in and taken over. She came to an intersection and took a left turn towards the communications systems.

Screens filled every wall in the comms centre. She locked herself in and searched through the views until she found the rest of her crew. She activated the audio feed, just in time to hear Raynor, his voice tinny and distant: "Lisa is still here, too. And I bet Salem will be going to the data core to try and protect whatever secrets they have been hiding here. That's where we need to go."

"Aww, how sweet," she said. "Here I was thinking you didn't care about me."

Everyone looked around.

"Lisa? Where are you?" Raynor said.

She scanned the other screens while she explained. There was no sign of Reen, but she did notice Salem making his way slowly towards the main reactor. There could only be one reason for him to go there, so she warned the crew. She needed more time to extract the *Altos-4* data.

While they went in search of Salem, Lisa kept looking for Reen. He didn't appear to be anywhere in the complex, which could have meant he was still on one of the ships. But then he wouldn't have this level of access to the *Altos-4* systems. For that, he would need a physical connection. The only place he could get that would be …

Lisa was shunted out of the construct, and Reen was right in front of her. His breath warmed her skin and chilled her spine. The fabricator robotoids hadn't just plugged her in to *Altos-4*, they had wrapped her in thick metal cords, restraining her arms and legs. She thrashed about, trying to get free. But she was firmly held in place.

"Well isn't this ironic," Reen said. "The first time we met, I was the one being restrained."

"Why are you doing this?"

"Because it's the only way to be free."

"By turning humanity into monsters like you did with Cliff?"

Reen scowled. "Humans are already monsters. Just look at this place. They cannibalised a cyborg to advance their research, enabling them to pick and choose the parts of our genetic code that best suited their grand designs. That's why the Colonies wiped out your kind. They don't want advancement, they want control."

"What about your former crewmates? Did you lure them here for revenge?"

"There is so much more to that ship than meets the eye. How have you been travelling with them for so long and not seen it? The reason I was invited to join them is because Rob needed my expertise to alter their DNA. It was essential in order to interact with the alien devices."

Lisa shook her head. "What are you talking about? Alien devices?"

"Look beyond the construct. There are datafiles about ancient technology that predates humanity. Devices that allow travellers to pass through walls, or gives the holder supernatural powers."

She located the files and flicked through them. The Star that Raynor had given her and the Artifact he had lost were both in there. The scientists on *Altos-4* were trying to locate and study more of them. She skimmed through the nodes and learned that the majority of technology, now commonplace in the colonies, came from these ancient devices. Now Reen wanted them, too.

More importantly, he didn't know she had the Star.

"Raynor hasn't told you about them, has he?" Reen ran his hand down the side of her face. "Of course not. You're there to spy on them. But you're upset that your Supreme Commander didn't tell you either."

Lisa turned her head. It was just about the only movement she could still manage. "What makes you think Raynor has them?"

"Your friend Cliff. I probed his mind and he revealed this to me. It's why I invited you here in the first place, enticing you with carefully placed hints of a captive that you couldn't ignore."

"Why are you wasting time telling me this?"

"Because we should be working together! Your kind was put down by the Colonies just like they tried to put me down. All for trying to cure myself of a terminal disease."

"But you weren't just trying to cure yourself, were you? You changed the dosages before Appel began the treatment without telling her."

Reen grinned. "I had a chance to drink from the Fountain of Light. I wasn't just going to stop at one sip."

A station-wide alert blasted through hidden speakers. "Reactor overload has been initiated. Please evacuate immediately."

"So what will it be? Will you join me or would you prefer to stay here?"

"Fine. Cut me loose and I'll help you," she lied.

Reen regarded her for a second, shook his head. "I wish I could believe you meant that."

"Reactor overload has been initiated. Please evacuate immediately."

"I certainly intend to," Reen said. "Enjoy the show."

He reached behind Lisa's head and yanked out the cluster of cables connecting her mind to *Altos-4*. The pain intensified, the room shrunk, Reen's face pixelated out as she lost consciousness.

When her systems rebooted, Reen was gone. Life Support and the restraints installed by the fabricators held her tight. Her only connection to the outside world was an interface in front of her displaying a direct feed of the hangar.

Reen wanted her to watch as everyone left her behind.

CHAPTER TEN
Phenomenology

Raynor turned the silver pin in his hands, watched as it caught the light. He knew he had seen it before, but it was as if his brain just wouldn't allow him to remember.

"Raynor!" Appel shouted.

He startled, looked up. Everyone was staring at him. "What?"

"We have to go," Persephone said. "Before the reactor explodes."

Raynor wondered how long he had spent examining the corrupted datafile. He pocketed the silver pin. "How long have we got?"

"My best estimate gives us twenty minutes," Rob said. "But it could easily go off in half that time."

Jake offered Raynor his blaster, the one used to shoot Salem only moment's before. Raynor took it by the handle, checked its charge and status indicator, then holstered it. "Jake, I never unlocked this weapon for you to use. How were you able to fire it?"

Jake shrugged. "Must be faulty."

Raynor raised an eyebrow, but Jake turned away, oblivious to Raynor's suspicion.

"We can make it to the ship in twelve," Raynor said. "Let's go!" They fell in behind as he headed for the exit.

Raynor set a fast pace, forcing Persephone to break into a run to keep up. Lights flickered throughout the eerily quiet labs on either side. His attention landed on the darkened interfaces lining the walls. This could only mean one of two things: Either Lisa had escaped and was already back on the ship or she was dead. Since his Link still had no signal, there was no way for him to find out. At least the essential systems were still online, sparing them the hassle of running in the dark with no oxygen.

They reached the damaged parts of the station, all that remained of the battle between the sentries, scientists and mutants. Raynor knew they were close now. This time, they passed through a processing area that would have served incoming and outgoing workers, the air still tainted by the smells of fire and death.

Jake rounded the corner and stopped in his tracks. Appel on his heel let out a gasp. Raynor stood silent as he looked up at the hulking semblance of their old shipmate, Reen. He looked younger, taller, stronger, and wore a smile like a weapon. He was wearing someone else's space suit printed with the *Elysium* emblem.

Reen's smile broadened into something that almost appeared genuine. "My friends," he said, holding his arms out wide. "So you did come to rescue me after all!"

Raynor exchanged a glance with Appel and Persephone.

"You have a bit of explaining to do," Raynor said. "For starters, what did you do to Cliff?"

The smile faded slightly, and Reen took a deep breath. He lowered his arms. "Is now really the time for this? We need to get out of here. I'll explain everything when we're back on the ship."

Persephone gripped her blaster, though she wasn't pointing it at Reen, yet. "We can do that once we're sure you're not a threat."

"A threat? Appel, tell them I'm not a threat."

Appel took a step back. "I know you altered the treatment. You're not the same person I knew … so what are you?"

"I made a few improvements of my own. All purely cosmetic, as you can see." Reen gestured at his altered complexion. "I don't see how a little vanity makes me dangerous."

"You lured us here," Raynor said. "Made Cliff into a monster, turned him against us."

Reen shook his head "Cliff found my stasis chamber, traded me to the mutants. The genetic alterations were his idea. He insisted that he be transformed into the ultimate evolution of humanity. Look, we really don't have time for this. You just need to trust me."

"How about you trust *me*," Appel suggested. "Let me sedate you. We'll take you back to the ship, verify that your enhancements don't pose a threat, then we can talk about what happens next." She slipped a medical disc out of a clip on her belt and took two cautious steps towards him.

"No," Reen said, his cheerful facade sliding away. "I won't let you put me back in stasis."

Persephone raised her blaster. "It's either that or a body bag."

The air around Reen started to shimmer and distort. Persephone dropped to her knees, blood running from her nose.

Raynor pulled his blaster, but as he took aim it crumbled to powder in his hand.

"You've always been quick to violence, Raynor. But your guns can't stop me now."

The space around Raynor buzzed with energy and time itself felt like it was being bent to Reen's will.

"What are you?" Raynor said through gritted teeth, his head pounding from the pressure of some invisible force.

"What I am," Reen said, "is something far beyond anything you could ever comprehend." He crossed the room in a flash and punched Raynor in the face.

Raynor groped the air. A coppery taste filled his mouth. His hand found Reen's space suit, so he used it to guide a swing of his own. Reen easily deflected the attack and replied with a kick to Raynor's ribs.

Raynor dropped to the deck, clutching his chest. Appel was behind Reen, reaching out with a med-disc.

Reen caught her wrist and turned to face her. "You think I don't know what that is? The failsafe is useless now my transformation is complete."

"If you're so far beyond comprehension now," Appel said, "what do you need us for? Why try to trick us into bringing you aboard?"

Reen shook his head. "I thought we were a team, you and I. What caused all of this hostility towards me? You wanted to save me, remember? None of this would have been possible without you."

"You used me! I took a huge risk to save your life and you exploited me. What did you think would happen if Swift hadn't intervened? That we would all just overlook that you weren't human any more?"

"I thought you would have joined me. I thought we had a connection."

Raynor looked around for the others. Persephone was still curled up on the ground in the foetal position, Jake and Rob were on their knees, incapacitated by the energy radiating from Reen. Appel was staring defiantly at Reen, still holding the failsafe disc.

"It's funny," Reen continued. "I can actually feel your loathing."

Appel didn't respond. She just stared unwaveringly. A tear rolled down her cheek and Raynor wondered what Reen was doing to her that he couldn't see. This was his chance. He spotted his blaster on the ground, the one he had seen disintegrate moments before. He fought the pain in his chest and grabbed the weapon, firing three rounds into Reen's back.

Appel collapsed into a heap and Reen calmly turned his attention back to Raynor, who fired two more shots. Reen swatted the high-velocity rounds away like they were plastic darts.

Reen lifted him up off the floor and slammed him against the wall. "You left me to fend for myself when the Prime came for me, and now I have become stronger than you can fathom. I'm going to enjoy killing you, Raynor."

Raynor felt his ribs and groaned. "How? You gonna talk me to death? Get on with it."

This is it, he thought. All the effort of living just to get beaten to death by a psychopath in a doomed space station. He coughed and a thousand tiny crimson orbs sprayed out in front of his face. A faint unease settled in, and he knew something was wrong. The droplets hung in the air, hardly moving. Reen seemed to be frozen in place like a statue, one of his arms drawn back ready to strike.

For a moment, Raynor thought he was already dead, and his mind was just drawing out his final moments. He sensed the Artifact's energy coursing through him, a spark of awareness, its power pulsating like a heartbeat in his pocket.

Reen's face was a snapshot of rage. Lips drawn back to show his clenched teeth, eyes fixed on Raynor. Every moment that passed, his fist drew ever closer to crushing Raynor's skull.

Raynor considered the blaster, realised it was still in his hand, and let it go. He didn't need it now. He used both hands to break Reen's hold and kicked with all his might. Reen was launched into the air with such force that Raynor thought the gravity had cut out.

Reality slipped away. He could see more than just light and matter; he could perceive energy, sound, and thought as though they were tangible things. It was like holding the tip of an iceberg; a small piece of a larger entity, but still connected somehow.

The Artifact wasn't quite a machine, but it wasn't a lifeform, either. He could sense an intelligence behind it, regarding him without emotion. At its core was something so incomprehensible that his brain struggled to conceive of it. The closest approximation he could think of was the opposite of a black hole. It was the beginning and the end of time and space. It was everything, everywhere, and nowhere, all at once.

The thing that was the Artifact regarded him for a moment. The weight of its attention was like staring at the sun, and the sun staring back.

You're not ready yet.

Raynor felt like the ground was pulled out from underneath him. The sensation of falling for eternity. It pushed him back. Back towards his body where Reen had just hit the wall. His awareness brushed by his friends, fleeing for their lives. He could feel their distress from having to abandon him. He recognised a familiar energy. It was the Star, and Lisa. She was still stranded somewhere in the depths of *Altos-4* and she was watching. She had seen everything.

Then, Raynor was trapped back in the flesh and blood prison that was his body once again. His senses felt muted, like he had gone deaf and blind to the greater universe that he was just connected to. His eyes didn't see enough, his thoughts weren't grand enough, his emotions didn't feel … enough.

He opened his mouth and closed it again. Clenched his hands into fists and opened them, getting his bearings in the cold reality of the processing area.

Coming back to life felt like dying, but at least his ribs felt better.

CHAPTER ELEVEN
Transference

The flashing red lights and pungent smell of burnt plastic brought Raynor back to reality. He was just a man, flesh and blood, sitting on the cold metal floor of a space station on the verge of destruction. He looked around, trying to remember what he was meant to be doing.

Reen laughed, still lying on the ground nearby. "So, you've finally worked out how to unlock it."

"I'm not going to let you take it," Raynor said. He looked around for his blaster, saw it nestled amongst the rubble, and reached for it. By the time he took aim, the airlock nearby cycled closed, covering Reen's escape.

Large windows at the far side of the battle-scarred room looked out over the cavernous ship docks. He stumbled over and pressed his hands against them. He could see his ship, still clamped to the air bridge.

Raynor sent a connection request to *Galaxy* and Diputs answered.

"Hey, don't leave without me," Raynor said.

"You'd better hurry, core stability is just about to reach critical."

The airlock was cycling too slowly. When it finally opened, his legs were just as cumbersome. The passage across the air bridge seemed to drag on for eternity.

Elysium had started its engines and was thrusting towards the exit.

Galaxy's pressure door opened promptly, and Raynor threw himself inside. Within the safety of the lobby, Appel was ready with a handheld scanner to check up on him.

Persephone shouted into her Link, "We've got him, get us out of here."

Lisa pinged his Link, now that he was back on the ship.

"Hey," he said between heavy breaths. "Are you coming or what?"

Lisa laughed. "I can't reach the Star. I'm trapped in here."

"Well … I guess you're fucked then."

"Raynor … Reen told me about the Artifact. I saw what just happened."

"Ahh …"

"When I get back to the ship, we need to talk. I want to hear the truth."

"But how? I thought you were trapped in there," Raynor said.

"I've still got a couple of tricks up my sleeve," she said, then dropped the connection.

The ship hummed as the gravity drive powered up. An interface on the wall displayed the forward view of the ship as they charged towards the narrow cave entrance. Compared to the slow and cautious entrance, their escape felt like a thrill seeker simulation, twisting left and right, narrowly missing certain death on each side.

An immense rumble reverberated through the ship, and Raynor thought they had struck something. Then the shockwave overtook them, shattering the cave walls and throwing them out into space.

The screen flared a blinding white, forcing Raynor to shield his eyes against the intense glare of the explosion. He could feel the heat, even through the ship's heavy shielding. *Galaxy* itself protested with a cacophony of alarms and flashing lights, indicating the erratic spin. Rocks and debris rattled against the hull as the light from the explosion faded. They had made it out in one piece.

A quick check of his Link told Raynor that Lisa wasn't aboard.

Lisa struggled to reach the Star in her pocket, but each time she fell short. She paused to catch her breath and took a moment to check her Link. The distress call hadn't made it out past the core's shielding.

Exhausted, she turned her attention to the monitor. Reen was confronting the *Galaxy* crew. The interface distorted and cut to Raynor, completely still. The distortion wasn't just a poor connection, it appeared to move around Raynor, and with an unjustified change in strength, he started fighting back. Whatever was happening to him, the effect was diminishing Reen's control over the rest of the crew, who started to recover. All but Raynor, who was staring at the ceiling in some sort of trance. Then the interface broke into static and distortion.

Lisa's mind raced, contemplating what Reen had told her about Raynor collecting alien devices. He had once lied to her about the Star, claiming it was burned out after their escape from the stolen battleship *Pywayrah*. It wasn't such a reach to believe he had also lied about losing the exigent cargo. Then what if he had orchestrated this entire ordeal? Could he have tipped off Swift so that Reen would be arrested and sent to *Altos-4*, giving him a reason to come here? Maybe even Swift was working with them, stranding her on their ship so that she was forced to go along with this plan to retrieve the *Altos-4* database, giving them access and knowledge to unlock the Artifact's secrets. There were too many possibilities and not enough evidence to support any of her suspicions. The only certainty was that if she was somehow able to get off this station before the reactors reached critical mass, she would need to go along with Raynor's plan and work with them to learn the truth.

She looked up at the sound of metal legs scuttling around the room. The fabricators had returned. "Hey. This place is going to blow up. Let me out of here!"

The robotoids circled, processing her request.

"Please," she added in a long drawn-out cry. A last-ditch effort to appeal to something that had no way of parsing emotions. A chill ran down her spine as one of the spiders climbed up her back.

"Let me go," she pleaded. Instead, her ears rang as it reconnected the primary data line, restoring her connection to *Altos-4*. It didn't want to let her go, it wanted her to fix the station.

While she was distracted, Raynor had awoken from his trance and returned to the ship with the others. Lisa opened a connection to Raynor. He accepted almost instantly. When his face appeared, he looked exhausted. She told him she knew everything. It felt strangely liberating, like they could finally be on the same side, in the know, as it were.

Returning her awareness physically, she sent out commands for the fabricators. New operational protocols, with one major directive: to release her. The fabricators went still for a moment, then sprung to life, cutting her arms free. She reached for the Star and pressed the activation trigger. Her body burst into light and she was free from the confines of the digital and physical worlds.

This wasn't the first time Lisa had travelled using the Star, but it was her first time flying solo. She remembered how Raynor had held her together by forming an awareness bubble around her. She collected all her thoughts, her awareness, her being, and pushed it through the station's optical infrastructure, and out into space.

She was faintly aware of two ships leaving *Altos-4* as it erupted behind them. For a single moment in time, she wondered what it would be like to just let herself go, to scatter her thoughts to the great abyss and be free forever. It was tempting, but she still had work to do. Now she knew about the Artifact, and the secret society pulling the strings. A bigger picture began to form in her thoughts; everything was connected. But it wasn't Raynor manipulating events for his own ends, it was this secret organisation who were starting wars and using the outlaws as a distraction.

Lisa peered into the ship. Diputs and Rob were in the control room. She grabbed onto their thoughts and used them to anchor her back into her physical form.

Her head spun as she came crashing back into her mind. No longer connected to *Altos-4*, no longer made of light and energy, just Lisa the cyborg. But when the crew looked at her in wonder and possibly fear, she didn't need anyone to tell her why.

"I know everything," she said as if it were an admission of guilt. Then, being conscious became too much. Her heavy eyelids closed and she embraced the loneliness of her own mind as she plunged into darkness. The last thing she felt as she fell to the deck o n *Galaxy* was that she was finally safe.

CHAPTER TWELVE
Company

The glow of the suspension field did little to hide Lisa's injuries. Still unconscious after three hours, the worst of her burns were covered with dermal regeneration pads, augmenting her self-repair nanites. Raynor floated in another suspension field while Appel scanned him.

"I feel fine," he said. "Do we really need to do all of these scans?"

"Yes," Appel said sharply.

"You're annoyed I didn't tell you," Raynor said.

Appel clenched her jaw. "We all have our secrets, I guess."

Rob flicked through a readout display on an interface. "We must try to understand how you were able to tap into those abilities, and why you can't seem to do it again."

"I don't think I had any agency in the matter," Raynor said.

"Is it safe to be talking about this in front of the cyborg?" Appel asked. "I thought you said it was a secret."

Rob looked over at the cyborg. "Her cognitive functions have been suspended as a precautionary measure whilst her nanites repair the damage. She won't remember any of this."

"It doesn't matter either way." Raynor squeezed the bridge of his nose. "She knows about the Artifact. She saw everything."

"You don't know what she meant by—"

"She *knows*, Rob. There is only one thing she is going to do when she wakes up. She's going to inform Swift, and we will be put on ice … just like Reen."

"She's had plenty of chances to rat us out, and she never did."

"This is different," Raynor said. "And this is our only chance to fix it. Before she wakes up. We need to erase the Artifact from her memory."

Rob laughed. "You can't simply reach in and pick out a single piece of information like that. Everything is intricately connected."

Raynor looked solemnly at Rob. "What about your device that can isolate memories? Surely someone as clever as you could figure out how to use it to remove some of those events."

"You're somewhat correct," Rob said, rubbing his chin. "We could use the Memory Isolator to *damage* the parts of her brain that store her most recent memories. But we would be removing everything from a certain point in time onwards."

"You can't be seriously entertaining this," Appel said. "We're not talking about deleting log entries here. What you're proposing is to maliciously inflict her with brain damage."

Raynor raised an eyebrow. "Will that cause ongoing issues?"

"I believe her nanites will be able to repair the tissue," Rob said. "But those memories will be lost."

"If that's the best we can do, then we need to at least try. We are so close to understanding exactly what this Artifact is. You heard her, Rob. She knows everything."

"You're not even giving her a chance to explain," Appel said. "You don't actually know how she is going to react."

"This is why Swift kept her here! I just think if there is a chance that we can safely cover our tracks, we should explore it."

"It will be a risky procedure," Rob said. "But given the current state that she's in, her internal systems should assume that the memory loss was part of the trauma. Our best option is to start from when she was hardwired into the *Altos-4* systems."

"That's perfect," Raynor said.

"I'm not going to be a party to this," Appel said. She took two steps towards the exit, then turned back and glared at Rob. "Don't mess this up."

Completely ignoring her, Rob brought up an active brain scan on the interface and studied it briefly. "That's interesting," he said. "This part of her brain is showing a massive conversion of genetic storage, which might suggest she has actually copied the entire *Altos-4* database, and it still exists inside her mind."

"What will happen to it if we start scrambling her recent memories? Can we get it out?"

"Not without killing her. She stored the information in a different part of her brain. Think of it as genetic cold storage." Rob scratched his beard. "But maybe we are looking at this wrong. Maybe we don't need to *get it out*. This could be a good thing for us. What she learned from the database might be enough to make her want to help us."

"It might, or it will be enough to condemn us."

Rob sighed.

Raynor paced the room. "But what if Appel's right? This is an extreme violation."

"Raynor," Rob rubbed his temples. "This is exactly what I feared when I created it!"

"Do we have a choice?"

Raynor chose the 'Orange' flavour on the interface of the colourful Organix dispenser in the common room. He liked Orange because the taste reminded him of a citrus drink he used to consume in his youth. He gulped it down like he hadn't had sustenance for rotations, dropped the used canister in the recycler and then took up a seat on one of the soft benches surrounding the garden area.

Everyone on the ship was gathered there to debrief after the events on *Altos-4*. Full-crew debriefs were rare. Especially with Lisa. In fact, it was by her request that they were all gathering to talk about what had happened.

He watched Lisa converse quietly with Appel while they waited for everyone to arrive. Only a couple of rotations ago she was riddled with punctures from where, as Rob surmised, the station had created connection points to all of her vital hardware. Now, there weren't even any noticeable scars, it was as if it never happened.

He looked over at Persephone, who must have noticed him staring at the cyborg, because she gave him a wink followed by a cheeky smile.

Diputs leaned on one of the planter boxes that enclosed the grassed area. He was the last one to join them.

Lisa stood, moved into the centre of the room and everyone's attention. Her gaze lingered on Raynor as she began.

"I know that I didn't start off on the best of terms with any of you, and my orders have always been to try to incriminate you for conspiring against the Colonies. My brain is still a bit of a mess after being connected to *Altos-4*, but I saw a glimpse of what is really going on. My mission here is a farce, and I'm being used just as much as all of you.

"*Altos-4* was charged with creating the next evolution of humanity. While we were in the labs, we all saw the illicit experiments. Cloning, genetic manipulation, as well as creating advanced weaponry and technology that is a long way ahead of anything we have seen before. That's where the mutants originally came from. What you didn't see is the cyborg they had mutilated and enslaved to process and advance their research." Lisa's voice quivered slightly. "The reason I am telling you all of this is because it's now clear to me that we have a common enemy. My kind was wiped out because of the fear of what we might have become. The threat we posed to humanity. The people behind *Altos-4* are still creating new monsters and manufacturing war between the Colonies. We have now interfered with these plans on a number of occasions, so you can bet that they will be watching what we do next. And I don't know what that should be … but whatever it is, we all need to be aware of the potential risks involved."

Raynor felt his tension ease, replaced with a sense of calm. There was no mention of the Artifact that he carried snugly in his jacket pocket. He gauged the rest of the room. It was unanimously fearful and uncertain.

Appel nervously bit her lower lip, Diputs folded his arms tight, Rob scowled, Persephone played with her necklace, Laz stared at his feet and Jake … Jake looked unnervingly calm.

"So what do we do now?" Persephone asked. "Can we even go back to Mars?"

"These people operate in the shadows," Lisa said. "But they have a long reach. If they want to bring us down, I'm not sure there is anywhere in the Colonies that we could hide."

"Luckily, *Altos-4* was isolated from the Colonies," Rob said. "Due to their secrecy, it's unlikely there will be anything left to pin this on us. Best thing we can do is return to Mars. We will go back to work and pretend everything is normal until you and Raynor come up with our next course of action."

With that, the group dispersed, a sullen forlorning radiated from them. Only Lisa remained. Raynor approached her and when no one else was in earshot, she said, "I know we haven't been very open in the past, but it's crucial we learn how to trust each other."

Raynor smirked. "So you're not going to go to Swift with this one?"

Lisa looked down. "Swift is many things … discreet is not one of them. I owe Swift my life. But I don't think I can count on him this time."

Lisa met Raynor's gaze. Her eyes were a perfect emerald green, and her skin was pale and soft. Reminding Raynor of the woman that she was. The human woman. This was the first time he was able to see past her cybernetic enhancements and the threat they posed.

"To be completely honest," she continued. "I don't really recall anything about what happened after those Fabricators made me part of the core. So I'm going to need you to fill me in on the rest of the events that led to us escaping."

Raynor studied her face, and nodded. "I'll write up a full account and send it to you."

Lisa smiled, and it seemed genuine enough.

In the seclusion of Rob's Bar, surrounded by interfaces and tubes of distilling liquid, Raynor cradled his glass of Cranium Rum. Each gulp did little to dispel the sullen vibes.

"Refill," he said.

Rob frowned and slid the bottle towards him. Raynor topped off his glass, spilling some of the golden liquid on the bench.

Diputs had been nurturing his one glass the entire time without taking so much as a whiff of it. "Does anyone want to, you know, say a few words?"

"This was all Reen's fault," Raynor grumbled.

Diputs sighed. "No. I mean, about Cliff and Abel. A dispersion is out of the question, given that no bodies were recovered. Besides, it's not like we can tell anyone how either of them actually died."

Rob leaned back in his chair. "Officially speaking, Abel died cycles ago. His family held a dispersion ceremony for him on Mars."

"Abel was a shitty engineer," Raynor said. "But an excellent friend. I don't much agree with what you did to him, Rob. If you ever pull any of that shit when my time's up, I'll use your blood to fry my circuits."

Rob gave him a crooked grin and sipped at his drink. "You're drunk."

"Abel gave his life for us," Diputs said. " Twice! I know you wanted to bring him back, Rob, but I think the best thing we can do to repay his sacrifice is to let him rest in peace."

Rob rubbed at his eyes. "I know … you're right. I wanted to give him a second chance at life, but the only kind of existence I could offer him was a window into reality. He was the technological equivalent of a ghost. Only I was the one that wasn't letting go."

Diputs patted him on the back. "You're an absolute mad man."

"The first time I met Cliff he yelled at me," Jake said.

Everyone turned to look at him.

"Cliff was alright," Raynor added. "When I first met him he was as green as a sapling. He didn't quite grasp the potential his position afforded him. But once he got the hang of it, he was a formidable ally."

Disputs smiled. "You could have asked him to set you up with a Peacekeeper's daughter and he would have given you that sly grin and asked what was in it for him."

Raynor raised his glass. "He would have made it happen, though." Then drank the remainder of what he hadn't spilt.

"Didn't you meet a Peacekeeper's daughter once?" Jake asked, looking at Rob.

"Yes," Rob said. "I met Peacekeeper Dalton's daughter on *M1*. She was lovely."

Diputs cleared his throat. "Can we try to stay on topic, please?"

"Yes, right," Rob said. "Cliff was one of us. Maybe not an official member of the crew, but he got it. He helped our cause of hunting for exotic treasures immeasurably. It won't be easy to replace him."

Diputs finally raised his glass to his lips and tipped it back. "To fallen comrades."

"Well it looks like we have our work cut out for us now," Jake said. "Reen is still out there somewhere, and then there are the Illuminis … does anyone else feel like we are a bit outmatched here?"

"None of it matters," Raynor said, staring at his glass. He let the silence hang. "What happened back there with the Artifact … it … showed me that there is something much larger than the universe."

"Like a god?" Jake asked.

"No, not like that. It was like some kind of higher plane of existence. Perhaps it's where the people who built the Star went. Some kind of ascension. The artifact is like one piece of something larger. It's an anchor to this reality."

Rob looked at him quizzically. "Alright, I'm cutting you off. I think you've had enough."

CHAPTER THIRTEEN
Report

Executor Zandr Barreth was enjoying a sunny afternoon lazing about by the pool. He shifted slightly in the suspension field holding him gently in a reclining position. Next to him a robotoid patiently hovered with a platter of cheese and wine; delicacies grown and processed right here in his own private oasis. He leaned over for a canapé and shielded his eyes from the light of the artificial sun glistening off the pool's calm surface.

His three-level grand estate was the only building on the immaculate rolling green hills spanning across the circular base of the cone-shaped space station. In the distance, behind the house, was a dull grey central column connecting the docks below all the way up to the control centre at the peak.

Reflections from the biosphere surrounding the station gave glimpses of the other twelve stations floating in low orbit around Lunar. Technically it was now eleven since the destruction of the *M1*.

Zandr heard a soft hum droning out from the central column and looked over the horizon to find its source. He squinted as he tried to locate the craft that zoomed towards his home. The chrome and glass sphere glistened under the artificial light as it flew towards him. It touched down gently on the pristine and unnaturally green grass. The Pod hissed as the front panel opened and a ramp extended, allowing the single occupant to exit the vehicle.

The visitor wore a white and silver Lunar Colony uniform. Cheeks covered in stubble, his eyes looked small and beady. He pulled out a microfibre cloth and wiped sweat off his forehead.

Zandr sent a mental command for the suspension field to push him to his feet. "Agent Fifty-eight, I presume?"

The Agent greeted him with an open palm facing upwards. "Yes, sir. You wanted me to bring you the sensor data in person?"

Zandr grinned. "Yes. You can never be too careful with digital communications. Even I can't ensure complete privacy."

The Agent's eyes widened. He reached into his coat for a data crystal. Zandr accepted it, and the information opened directly in front of him. Telescopic imaging from three rotations ago overlaid on an updated capture, which clearly showed one less asteroid in the centre of frame. He flicked through the different visual and radiation spectrums, but the point was clear. *Altos-4* was gone.

"How did this happen?"

"We don't know, sir. Mars sent a high-value asset to the station with a military escort. A UAEN destroyer was the last ship to have contact with *Altos-4*. The crew reported that the drop was completed with nothing out of the ordinary, then the ship completely disappeared."

Zandr skimmed through the included data on the crew profiles. "Disappeared, huh?"

They were mostly mid-level nobodies. None posed even a slight risk to a facility such as *Altos-4*. He turned his attention to the Cargo; Genetic modification profile, extremely volatile. The subject had been put in stasis and sent for dissection and study at the labs. He shuddered to think of the sorts of insane abominations they were cooking up over there. It was only a matter of time before something turned on them.

"Clean this up," Zandr said, finally. "I don't want any record that this project ever existed."

"Yes, sir. Understood."

Agent Fifty-eight turned towards the Pod.

"Wait, there's one more thing," Zandr continued. "We're about to move on to the next phase. I need you to go to the Saturn Alliance Colony. They are on the brink of war and we need someone to push them over the edge. Think you can handle that?"

"Sir, I believe The Nexus has already sent an Agent to mediate their appeasement—"

"Then you will need to *replace* them." Zandr raised an eyebrow.

The agent gave him a curt nod. "Then it will be done."

About The Author
Chris Masterton

Chris is a space nerd, tech enthusiast, and sci-fi author. He enjoys exploring themes such as the future of humanity, artificial intelligence, and the impact technology has on society. Chris has a background in software and graphic design.

Connect with Chris:

- www.chrism.au

- goodreads.com/chrismasterton

About The Author
Steven Dutch

Steven Dutch was born in Auckland, New Zealand but grew up in Sydney, Australia. He would consider himself a foodie, and enjoys most cultures' foods. He works a day job as a Cyber Security Service Delivery Manager and enjoys everything scientific and technological, which bleeds over into his writing often. He has always been fascinated by science fiction and magic, thinking there is a fine line between the two and enjoys writing stories meshing and melding the two together. He has been writing for many years and has completed several writing seminars and courses.

Connect with Steven:

- goodreads.com/stevendutch

History of Sol

H istory of Sol is an action/adventure sci-fi novella series set in the distant future.

Find out about the latest releases and where you can meet the authors using our social media links:

- historyofsol.com

- facebook.com/history.of.sol

- instagram.com/historyofsol

- twitter.com/historyofsol

Glossary

- **Observer:** Spy/Intelligence gatherer

- **Executor:** High ranking Illuminis agent

- **Peacekeeper:** The highest level of Nexus administration

- **Illuminis:** A collective of influential people in the Colonies

- **Datafile:** An automated file system that gathers and sorts all information in the Nexus

- **Data Crystal:** A small quartz disk that serves as a mobile data storage device

- **Habitat:** A self-contained living area on smaller spacecraft

- **Holo:** Holographic Interface

- **Interface:** Computer

- **Link:** Communication device / Mobile personal interface

- **Mitron:** Microscopic unit of measurement

- **Millitrons:** Tiny unit of measurement

- **Centron:** Small unit of measurement

- **Metron:** Medium unit of measurement

- **Kiltron:** Large unit of measurement

- **Nexus:**

- **a) name -** The governing body uniting all of the colonies under the 'Nexus Treaty'

- **b) technology -** A colony-wide shared communication and data system

- **Node:** A subsystem component of a Nexus or Datafile

- **Organix:** Liquid sustenance

- **Outlaw:** A general term used to denote people without Value

- **Robotoid:** A small self-mobilised robot

- **Fabricator:** Specialised repair robotoids unique to *Altos-4*

- **Alchemic Manifestors:** molecular printers capable of the transmutation of matter

- **AST (Fusion Reactor):** Advanced Superconducting Tokamak

- **M1:** Matias Network Orbital Space Station 1 (Lunar Colony)

- **MLE:** Mars Logistics Entity

- **MSCF:** Mars Space Combat Fleet

- **UAEN:** United Advancement Entity Navy

- **Rotation:** The time it takes for Mars to complete one rotation around its axis

- **Sub-Cycle:** 1/24th of a Cycle

- **Cycle:** The orbital period of Mars to pass once around Sol

- **Tectanium:** A super-strong metal derived from Titanium and enhanced with nano-tech

- **The Artifact:** A small shard of unknown material and origin

- **The Star:** A quantum state transference with a conduit of antimatter resonance (converts matter into light for brief periods of time)

- **The Terranean Expanse:** An asteroid belt between Lunar and Venus

- **Luume:** A city on Enceladus, sixth largest Moon of Saturn

- **Value:** Economic recognition level

www.ingramcontent.com/pod-product-compliance
Lightning Source LLC
Chambersburg PA
CBHW061030100726
47911CB00001B/27